THE
BILLIONAIRE'S
SECRET KISS

The Winters Saga
Book Six

IVY LAYNE

GINGER QUILL PRESS, LLC

Contents

Also by Ivy Layne

THE HEARTS OF SAWYERS BEND

Stolen Heart

Sweet Heart

Scheming Heart

Rebel Heart

Wicked Heart

THE UNTANGLED SERIES

Unraveled

Undone

Uncovered

THE WINTERS SAGA

The Billionaire's Secret Heart (Novella)

The Billionaire's Secret Love (Novella)

The Billionaire's Pet

The Billionaire's Promise

THE BILLIONAIRE CLUB

CHAPTER ONE
ELLA

I was late. I'm never late.

Twenty minutes to get to campus. I had a two o'clock appointment with my thesis advisor. Oliver was trying to see if he could get me put back on our project even though I wasn't currently enrolled in the Master's program.

It was a long shot, and I didn't want to blow it by being late.

I hated to interrupt a meeting, but I'd told my bosses I needed a few hours off this afternoon, and I had to hand over my charge before I left. Cradling baby Rosie against my shoulder, I nudged the door to the office open with my hip, saying, "I'm so sorry to interrupt, but it's one forty and—"

I looked up, and my breath froze in my lungs.

Noah Endicott was sitting across the room. He lounged in the chair opposite Vance's desk, his brown eyes wide with surprise and fixed on mine.

"Ella?"

That was all he said. Just *Ella.*

I wasn't much better. I didn't say anything. I just stared.

It was Noah, but not *my* Noah. My Noah wore faded T-shirts with geeky engineering jokes. My Noah's dark hair was long enough to fall into his eyes. My Noah had a sweet smile.

My Noah had broken my heart.

The man in front of me may have looked like my first love, but I doubted they had anything in common.

This Noah had short hair and lines around his eyes.

This Noah wore an expensive designer sweater instead of a T-shirt and hoodie, though the faded jeans and black-and-white Converse high-tops were heartbreakingly familiar.

"Ella?" Maggie asked, concern heavy in her voice. "Are you okay? Do you and Noah know each other?"

I looked at my bosses and tried to get my head back in gear. Vance and Magnolia were both staring at me with concern. I needed to get myself together before they decided I was losing it. Vance and Maggie had hired me as Rosie's nanny a few months before, and thanks to them, I might be able to save up enough money to go back to school.

That was my plan. Work for Vance and Magnolia. Save every penny. Go back to school.

Noah had no part in any of that.

"I'm so sorry, Maggie. I thought Rosie would fall asleep on her walk, but she's still up, and I have to go."

Maggie stood and scooped the baby out of my arms. "I lost track of time, Ella, or I would have come to get her. Don't worry about it. We're good. Why don't you take the rest of the day off after your meeting?"

"Thanks so much," I said, half over my shoulder, as I escaped the room without another word. Behind me, I heard Noah say, "Ella! Ella, wait!"

No way. I'd spent enough of my life waiting for Noah Endicott. I'd learned my lesson.

As fast as I could without running, I walked down the hall to get my purse and keys from the kitchen. A few more seconds and I'd be in my car on the way to school.

My purse was not on the counter where I left it. Dammit. I didn't have time for this.

My heart thundering in my chest, I scanned every flat surface in the kitchen for my red purse and silver key ring.

I wasn't sure whether I was rushing to my appointment or just desperate to escape Noah.

Noah.

How was Noah at Vance and Magnolia's? He was in California. As far as I knew, he hadn't been back to Georgia since three months before we'd broken up.

Why was he here now?

Vance was an artist, but he was also an angel tech investor on the side. He'd met Magnolia when he hired her as his assistant, and they'd gotten married a few months before. Vance and Maggie met with a lot of guys like Noah, but there were angel investors in California. Silicon Valley was filled with them. Why was he in Atlanta? Why was he *here*?

Maybe after what had happened, no one would talk to him out there.

It didn't matter. Noah was the past. My future depended on doing my job and staying in Oliver's good graces so I could get back into my program when I could afford to pay for it.

Focus, Ella.

Where the hell did I leave my purse?

An image of the built-in bench beside the front door flashed in my mind. Yes! Rosie had been crying when I'd shown up that morning, and I dropped my purse and keys on the bench to get to her so Maggie could finish making breakfast without a screaming baby in her arms.

I whirled for the front hall and bumped smack into Noah. His hands came up to my shoulders, holding me in place. Up close, he looked tired and older. He smelled the same. Clean. Like the ocean and freshly-cut grass.

Scent memory is a killer. Just like fresh-baked chocolate chip cookies always brought me right back to my mom's kitchen, that unique combination of salty sea and green grass meant Noah. My brain and heart stuttered, remembered love flooding through me.

No.

No.

I stepped back, jerking my shoulders out from under his grip.

"I have to go," I said.

Noah's hand shot out and closed over my wrist. "Ella, wait. We have to talk."

"No, we don't. There's nothing to say. I have to go. I'm going to be late."

Noah shifted to block my path to the door. "Please, Ella. If you can't talk now, have dinner with me."

Was he crazy? I didn't want to be in the same room with Noah Endicott, much less have dinner with him.

"No! Noah, I don't know why you're here, and I don't care. We don't have anything to say to each other anymore. Please just leave me alone."

"I can't do that," Noah said, shifting again to block my exit. "I know you're mad. You probably hate me. But I need to talk to you. There are things I need to explain—"

"There's no point," I said, no longer confused as to

whether I was rushing to my appointment or running from Noah.

I was definitely running from Noah. Just being this close to him had my emotions in turmoil, my stomach tight and chest hollow with remembered pain.

I'd loved him so much. I couldn't do this. I didn't want to be anywhere near him. Especially not now.

"There's every point," Noah insisted. "Look me in the eyes and tell me you don't still have feelings for me, and I'll walk away. I swear."

I raised my eyes to his, trying not to flinch at the heat and longing in his bittersweet chocolate gaze. I'd always loved his eyes.

"I don't have any feelings for you, Noah," I said.

"Liar."

Noah raised his hands to cup my face, sliding one hand back to bury his fingers in my hair, cradling my skull and tilting my face up to his. His touch was gentle, light enough that I could have easily stepped away.

I didn't. A part of me wanted to. Wanted to run as fast as I could and never see Noah again. But the second he touched me, I froze, just like I had when I'd seen him sitting in Vance's office.

His touch was so familiar. The way he held my face, the stroke of his thumb over my cheek. I had plenty of time to dodge his kiss. I don't know why I didn't do it.

"Ella," he whispered, his lips so close they stroked mine as they moved. His breath smelled like lemon and mint. He'd always loved chewing those lemon mint candies. My body swayed into his, drawn by history and a love I'd never quite been able to kill.

When his tongue grazed my bottom lip, I opened to him out of reflex. Two years. It had been two years since I'd seen

Noah, but my body had forgotten nothing. And apparently, it hadn't learned any lessons from Noah's desertion.

One touch and all I wanted was him.

His mouth moved over mine, sucking on my bottom lip, then my top, before he tilted my head back and dove into the kiss. One arm went around my waist, pulling me tight to his body. Without thinking about it, my hand rose to curl around the back of his neck, holding him close.

I'd always loved kissing Noah. He knew what I wanted before I did. When to take me deeper. When to back off. How to tease me until I was dying to touch him.

I heard myself moan as he backed me into the kitchen island, pulling his mouth from mine to graze his lips along my chin. He nipped the side of my neck in that spot that always made me shiver. My hand curled into his hair, guiding his mouth down to my collarbone.

Noah was already on his way.

My hips rolled into his, my skin flushed, my body heating from head to toe at the feel of his hard cock pressing into me. I hooked my leg around him, dragging his thickness against me, grateful I was wearing a skirt when he gripped the back of my knee with strong fingers before sliding his hand up my bare thigh to close around the swell of my ass.

His teeth closed over the tendon in my neck, a bite of possession that wouldn't leave a visible mark but burned through me to my core. When his fingers grazed the edge of my practical cotton panties, I didn't push him away. I dropped my head back and moaned.

I wasn't surprised I was wet. One fingertip slid beneath my underwear to trace my pussy, easily gaining entrance to my body. Two years since anyone had touched me there. No other man had come close. No other man was Noah. Raw pleasure spiked through me when he pressed that fingertip into my clit. Just the way I liked it.

His tongue stroked across my collarbone, and I shuddered in his arms.

"Ella," he breathed into my skin. "Ella, baby, I missed you so much."

His words were a bucket of ice water, annihilating the cloud of lust messing with my brain.

I jerked away and shoved hard, rocking Noah back on his heels just enough to get free. I wiped the back of my hand against my mouth as if I could erase the kiss, pressing my thighs together to quiet the needy hum between my legs.

Noah was everywhere, the imprint of his hands on my skin, his scent in my nose.

Fucking Noah.

No. I was *not* fucking Noah.

He reached out and grabbed my hand. "Ella, please—"

I wrenched my arm out of his grip, threw it back, and punched him as hard as I could.

Noah let out a yowl of pain, his hands going to his nose. He drew one away and looked at it. Bright red blood stained his fingers.

"You hit me!"

"I'm sorry." I was lying. I wasn't sorry.

As if reading my mind, Noah said, "I had it coming."

"Did I break it?" I couldn't help asking.

"Did you mean to?"

"No! I didn't mean to hit you at all. I didn't mean to kiss you either."

"Now that you did, now that I have to go back into that meeting with a bloody nose will you at least go to dinner with me?"

"No."

That kiss was proof I couldn't be anywhere near Noah. I had no willpower where he was concerned. And no reason to trust him.

"I'm not giving up, Ella."

Exasperated, my heart bleeding, I pushed past him, saying, "I have to go, Noah. I can't be late. Please don't tell Vance and Maggie about this."

Behind me, I heard him say, "Later, Ella. I'll find you later. This isn't over."

But it was. It had been over for months before we'd finally broken up. Noah wasn't mine anymore. I'd moved on. I wasn't going back.

I couldn't afford to.

CHAPTER TWO
ELLA

Noah didn't try to stop me as I snatched up my purse and keys and ran for my car. He was probably too busy cleaning up his bloody nose. I didn't feel guilty about punching him. I shouldn't. He'd been right—he did have it coming.

He was lucky a punch to the nose was all he'd gotten from me.

I jumped in my car, threw on my seatbelt, and sped down the driveway.

I was going to be late. If traffic was on my side, it wouldn't be too bad. And if I could find a parking place.

My lips burned, swollen and hot. Why had I kissed him? He'd started it, but that was no excuse.

I'd kissed him back.

Why? I didn't want Noah. I didn't.

He'd broken my heart. Shattered me. He didn't deserve a second chance. I wasn't going to give him one.

Unbidden, an image of Noah the day we'd met popped into my mind. He'd been in my Introductory Media Computation class. I was a freshman. He was a sophomore.

I grabbed a seat two down from his, got out my notebook, and realized I'd lost my pen somewhere in the rush between classes.

I'd turned to ask if he had one I could borrow, and those bittersweet chocolate eyes had me. Back then, his thick hair had been short, but not like today. Whoever was cutting his hair now, they knew what they were doing. It might be shorter than I liked, but it showed off his bone structure beautifully.

The day we'd met, he'd had one of those utilitarian haircuts that boys get when they don't know any better. He'd been gangly, too tall for a body that hadn't really filled out yet. He'd flushed a little when he lent me the pen, but he worked up the nerve to ask my name. When he complimented my Buffy T-shirt, my cheeks had turned pink to match his.

After class, he'd asked me to get a coffee together. I said yes.

We were together all the time after that. Noah was smart and funny, and he seemed to think that I was the most gorgeous, interesting creature on the planet.

I fell hard.

Our relationship went backward. I was already head over heels in love with him by the time he made it past first base. Neither of us had a whole lot of experience. I was a virgin, and so was Noah, though he turned bright red and stuttered a little when I got him to admit it.

By the time we finally had sex, I was sure Noah was the only man I'd ever love. He swore he felt the same.

You'd think the sex would've been bad, considering neither of us had any idea what we were doing. But Noah and I had always been good at talking, and we'd learned together. He was patient and a good listener. By the time we'd had a few months' practice, sex with Noah was amazing. We both took classes that summer so we could stay on campus together, and I think we spent more time in bed than out of it.

Noah was my everything. My first love, my best friend. He was set to graduate a year ahead of me, and we'd both planned to go to grad school. Everything was good until Noah got an offer from Caltech that he couldn't turn down. A full ride to one of the most competitive master's programs in the world.

We were so naïve, so certain everything would be fine with him across the country. As we'd both originally planned, I was set on the master's program at Georgia Tech. I didn't have anything against moving to California, but not yet. Noah's program at Caltech was only two years. He accepted, promising he'd be back as soon as it was done.

Instead, he developed a pioneering program to target rogue drones, dropped out of Caltech to start his own company, licensed the program to the military, and made a ton of money. He was on the cover of *Wired*, *Fast Company*, and a whole bunch of other magazines and newspapers.

By then, he'd gotten bad about returning my calls. He claimed he was working non-stop on a new version of his drone software, as well as expanding the company and licensing other, related software. Suddenly, he had employees and clients and so many other things more important than a girlfriend across the country.

When he'd no-showed my college graduation, I'd been so hurt I'd lost my temper.

We'd been fighting, off and on, for months. Mostly about his preoccupation with Endicott Technologies and his changing plans for the future. He kept pushing me to apply to Caltech, but the program I wanted at Georgia Tech was unique. There wasn't anything at Caltech like it. I'd worked too hard to walk away from everything. California wasn't on my roadmap until I finished school.

The day of my college graduation finally arrived, and Noah's travel plans were still uncertain. He left me with the impression that he might show up. I spent the day with a pasted-on smile to appease my parents, craning my neck to look over the crowds for Noah.

He never made it.

Heartbroken, I'd sent him a single text.

I can't do this anymore. I think we'd both be happier apart.

I never heard anything back. Three weeks later, Noah was featured on a tech blog, the picture taken at a Silicon Valley release party. Noah wore skinny jeans and a tailored shirt. A blonde model was draped on his arm.

I'll admit it. I cried over that picture. That one, and the one after it, and the one after that. Noah moved on from me without a hitch in his step, replacing me with a series of interchangeable models, actresses, and other semi-famous women happy to be on the arm of Silicon Valley's newest tech billionaire.

For a while, Noah was riding high, and I was just the girl he left behind. Then, out of nowhere, an old friend came out of the woodwork to topple Noah from his throne. Phillip Martin, a guy we both knew from our undergrad classes, hit the media with the claim that Noah had stolen the code he'd used for Endicott Tech's flagship software.

A lawsuit followed a few days later. Noah was on the covers of all the same magazines again, this time as the villain. Speculation ran rampant, everyone picking sides, fingers pointing at Noah as a thief and a liar. There were no more pictures of Noah escorting models and actresses. Now it was Noah, drunk at a club with a porn star. Noah fighting with a reporter. Noah walking out of a meeting, scowling at everyone.

I called him one night, right after I saw a picture of him online, his eye blackened from a fight at a bar. He'd looked so alone. So lost.

He'd answered right away, even sounded grateful for my call. For a few weeks, we'd talked. Not every day, and never for long. I'd started to hope we might get back together. My hope didn't last long. One night, I called, and a woman's voice sounded in the background.

"Do you have company?" I'd asked, trying not to jump to conclusions.

My heart sank at the guilt in his voice when he said, "Uh, kind of. She—"

"You have a date?" My voice had wobbled, my total lack of cool humiliating. We weren't together. Noah had a right to date. I'd just thought . . . I'd thought a lot of things. Things that were only true for me.

"Can I call you back later?" Noah had asked. At least he'd had the grace to sound sheepish. Had he known what I was thinking? That I'd been hoping we were finding our way back to each other?

He did call me back. More than once. I didn't answer.

I needed a clean break. I couldn't be friends with Noah. The agony at hearing a woman's voice in his apartment had shown me that. If we weren't together, I was better off on my own. I tried to ignore the news reports as Noah settled out of court with Phillip Martin.

He'd moved on, and Endicott Technologies continued to pop up in the news cycle, but I ignored it all. Noah was out of my life for good.

If I hadn't had school, I would have fallen into a dark pit

of ice cream and chick flicks and weepy nights home alone. I still had my share of those, but I'd gotten into the master's program at Tech that I'd wanted and had hit the ground running. I was a Computer Science major and Music minor in undergrad, and my master's program was a combination of the two disciplines, focused on ways to use music and programming together in STEM courses to ignite the imaginations of coders and artists alike.

It was fascinating and exciting, and I loved using our projects with real students, seeing their eyes light up, the way the kids into programming suddenly got the creativity possible in coding and watching the kids into music find new ways to compose using code.

I loved my master's program almost as much as I'd loved Noah.

Now, I had neither. Though there was the tiniest of chances that I could get my foot back in the door at school if Oliver had managed to swing an exception.

The fates were smiling on me, at least when it came to parking spaces. I found one not too far from the CS building, maneuvered my car against the curb, and jumped out, only a few minutes late.

I raced down the street and up the stairs into the building, bypassing the elevator and taking the stairs to the third floor two at a time. I was gasping for breath when I knocked on Oliver's office door.

"Sorry I'm late," I said when he answered.

"That's all right, Ella, it's only a few minutes," he said in a gentle tone that would have been reassuring if I hadn't been afraid of what it meant. Oliver wasn't usually gentle. Brusque, impatient, and mostly nice about it, but not particularly gentle with his students. He expected us to work our asses off and be the best.

He gestured to the seat opposite his desk and said, "Take a load off, Ella. It feels like I haven't seen you in months."

That was because he hadn't.

A year before, shortly after second semester had started, I'd received notice from the bursar's office that my tuition had not been paid. I'd been fortunate so far that my parents had covered a lot of my undergrad and master's tuition, supplemented by a few small grants.

I'd worked through college, waiting tables and tutoring to make up the difference. I knew I'd paid my share of spring tuition, and I'd been able to get a small grant to cover another chunk, but my parents had agreed to foot the bill for the rest. I'd figured it hadn't been a big deal—maybe they just forgot to send in the check.

I went home for the weekend and discovered there was no mistake. A 'For Sale' sign sat in the yard of my childhood home. My mother's car was missing, and my father's had been traded in. Inside the house, everything of value was gone.

I don't know how they thought they would keep it a secret, but my father tearfully confessed that he'd lost his job over a year before and instead of telling anyone, had pretended to keep going to work while borrowing more and more money to finance their lifestyle.

He swore he hadn't meant for it to get so out of control, that he'd been interviewing and had been sure he'd find something else. Until suddenly, it was too late, and everything was gone.

I managed to get a small loan to cover the gap for spring tuition. Since I'd already started and I couldn't get a refund, it seemed smarter to find a way to finish. I was still paying off that loan. It hadn't seemed like much money at the time, but when every penny is going to rent and food, even a small loan is nearly impossible to pay off.

I hadn't enrolled again. I wouldn't. Not until I could pay my tuition upfront. Until Vance and Maggie had hired me, I'd been couch surfing in a very crowded apartment, waiting tables and trying to save for tuition to finish school. Between my share of the rent, the loan, and saving, things had been tight. Very tight.

I tried not to be angry at my parents. Their change in circumstance had been a lot rougher on them than it had been on me. My dad managed to find another job at half the salary he was used to. They'd gone from a nice suburban house to a tiny condo. My parents were doing the best they could, and every time they asked how I was, I smiled and told them I was fine.

I wasn't fine. I missed school painfully. Losing Noah was bad enough, but leaving school on top of it—I felt like a shell of myself most days. More than anything, I just wanted to get back to how things were. I wanted to finish school, get a job in my field, and move on with my life.

I was tired of being stuck in between, spinning my wheels while I saved money and waited for things to change.

"Ella, how have you been?" Oliver asked, again in that gentle tone that made me nervous.

I shrugged. "I've been okay. I think I told you I got a job as a nanny for Vance and Magnolia Winters. That's made things easier, and it comes with a place to live so I can save more money. And I've been doing some freelance work here and there for WGC. That helps too."

"WGC? Winters Gaming Corp.? That's not really your field of expertise. How'd you get that gig?" Oliver steepled his fingers under his chin and studied me as if I were a puzzle he wanted to solve. I'd seen him aim that look at students before. It was a little unnerving, but I knew he meant well.

"Do you know Emily Winslow and Jo Miller? They graduated last year." At Oliver's nod, I went on. "We're pretty good friends, and they're dating Holden and Tate Winters. I've gotten to know them, and when they heard what happened, they offered me some freelance work. I'm pretty sure they could get someone more qualified or someone in-house, but what they've been sending me isn't too advanced. If I had another option, I wouldn't take it, but . . ."

I trailed off. I knew, and both Holden and Tate knew, that I was not their best option for the programming work they'd been sending me. I was pretty sure they had employees in-house to do it, though they claimed they were continually short-staffed and under pressure to make deadlines.

I didn't push because I needed the money. They'd offered to lend me the cash for tuition. For that matter, so had Vance and Maggie. I'd wanted to take their offers so badly I could taste it. I wanted to be back in school. But I wasn't borrowing any more money.

I'd already learned how easy it was to take a loan and how hard it was to pay it back.

My field was fascinating and exciting, but it wasn't lucrative. Not unless I ended up developing some break-through app that sold like crazy. It could happen, but it wasn't likely. If I were lucky, I'd find a job in academia, which would be fine with me. It would be great. But it wouldn't necessarily leave me in a position to pay off loans.

I'd seen firsthand the devastation that debt could wreak. Every time I was tempted to take one of my friends' offers, I thought about my mom, carefully decorating her one-bedroom condo with the few things she'd been able to salvage from her former life, pasting on a bright smile and acting like everything was okay when inside, I knew it was killing her.

I wasn't going there. I was not going to borrow a goddamned dime. I would wait, and I would save every penny until I could do it myself.

"That's good news, Ella. It sounds like you're making some headway on the tuition front," Oliver said encouragingly. "I can't tell you how much I'm looking forward to having you back in class. It's not the same around here without you."

I didn't have to try hard to read between the lines. "But you can't let me volunteer in the program until I'm officially enrolled," I said, trying to keep my voice even.

Slowly, Oliver shook his head. He didn't try to hide the regret in his eyes. "I'm sorry, Ella. I tried. I'd love to have you back, if not as a student, then as a volunteer. But the department consensus was that any position on the project had to be held by a current student. The experience is too valuable to give away if it can't be applied to the degree. I can promise you that as soon as you can pay tuition, you have a place here. I don't want you to lose hope."

"I understand," I said, swallowing hard. I'd known it was a long shot. It meant a lot that Oliver had volunteered to ask. There were students who'd give anything to work on this project, and I wasn't a student anymore.

"Have you looked into grants again? Maybe there are better loan options than there were last time?" Oliver asked encouragingly.

I shook my head. "None of the grants I'm eligible for would cover enough of the cost," I said. "And I'm not going to get another loan. I'm still paying off that last semester. I should be clear of it by next month, but if I borrow enough to pay for tuition, I'll be in a hole forever."

"I understand," Oliver said, coming to his feet and setting a hand on my shoulder briefly before turning to the door. I stood, too. I knew that he meant it. He knew what had happened with my parents, knew why I wouldn't get a loan.

"Thanks for trying, Oliver," I said, heading out the door.

"Anytime, Ella. Stay in touch. As soon as you think you'll be back, let me know."

"I will," I promised.

I ran down the stairs to the lobby of the building and pushed open the doors, the crisp November air bringing tears to my eyes. Maybe it wasn't the air. I'd known Oliver probably couldn't get me back in the program, even as a volunteer. I hadn't realized how much I'd been counting on it.

I strode down the block to my car, my head down. Sliding behind the wheel, I put my keys in the ignition but didn't turn them. I leaned forward, resting my forehead against the steering wheel, and cried.

CHAPTER THREE
NOAH

I couldn't believe Ella punched me.

Okay, maybe I could.

Our breakup hadn't exactly been amicable. In retrospect, I'll admit that was mostly my fault. At the time, I hadn't seen it that way.

Aware that my potential investors were waiting for me in the other room, I grabbed a paper towel and wet it at the sink, hoping I could clean up my bloody nose before they realized what had happened.

I'd already fucked things up with Ella. I didn't need to fuck this deal up, too. My employees depended on me to get the funding we needed to finish development in time for our big payday. I wasn't going to let them down.

What they didn't realize, what nobody knew, was that I wasn't just here to sweet-talk Vance and Maggie Winters into investing in Endicott Technologies.

I was here for Ella.

I cleaned the blood off my face, determined that my nose had stopped bleeding, and walked back into Vance and Maggie's office. Maggie had moved to sit beside him at the desk, and their heads were together, leaning over his laptop screen as they spoke in hushed voices. The baby was asleep in a portable crib in the corner of the room.

Vance and Maggie made a striking couple. When he wasn't investing in up-and-coming tech companies, Vance Winters was a renowned sculptor. He looked the part with long blonde hair he wore in a low ponytail, a ton of tattoos, and a generally laid-back approach to life.

Maggie had originally hired on as his business manager. She was said to be sharp, with an excellent head for business. Between the two of them, they didn't miss much. In contrast to Vance's relaxed style, both times I'd met her, Maggie had been brisk and efficient. I was a man, so I didn't miss that she was gorgeous, but she didn't dress to play it up, and she never flirted.

She looked up when I walked back into the room, appraising me carefully. Any hope I had that we could get back to business went up in a puff of smoke when she said quietly, "How do you know Ella?"

Vance sat back and waited, along with Maggie, for my answer. I didn't even think about lying. I promised to keep the kiss a secret, but I wasn't going to screw this deal by being dishonest about Ella.

"We dated for three years in college," I said, keeping my voice low, so I didn't wake the sleeping baby.

"And?" Vance prompted.

"And what?" I asked, crossing my arms over my chest.

"You rushed out of here after her," Maggie said, "and it didn't look like she wanted to talk to you."

I did not want to do a postmortem of my breakup with Ella. Not with anyone, but definitely not with the two people I needed to invest in my company.

"Is this relevant?" I asked, trying to deflect.

"It is if you want our money," Vance said. "This isn't just about numbers, Noah. We know what you've done so far with your company. We understand the potential of what you're developing. We also understand that you want to keep control of your Endicott Tech. You've designed the software to disable an enemy drone in seconds. But that's not new. Other companies have that. No one has been able to crack how to do it and still comply with the FAA's laws in the US. If your current tests pan out, you stand to make a ton of money. We'd love to get our hands on some of that money, and we don't want control of Endicott Tech to get it, which is a much better deal than you'll get from any other investor out there. But we have reservations."

"You're talking about the lawsuit," I guessed.

That fucking lawsuit. Someday, I was going to kill Phillip Martin. He'd tried to destroy me more than once. In college, he'd accused me of cheating. That hadn't gone far. I had witnesses to prove my innocence. Unfortunately, when it came to the lawsuit, Philip had been smart. I knew I hadn't stolen a goddamned thing. That didn't mean shit when Phillip had a stack of evidence that made it look like I did.

"Yes," Vance agreed. "Normally, we wouldn't have anything to do with a company, a founder, under suspicion of theft."

"The case was settled with no admission of guilt," I said flatly. I was so fucking sick of defending myself against this bullshit.

"I understand you paid Phillip Martin quite a bit of money," Maggie said evenly.

"I did," I agreed. "Per the settlement, I'm barred from disclosing the details. But that payment was about moving past the case and getting my company, my people, back to work. We needed to put our budget into development, not lawyers."

A priority Phillip had been counting on when he brought the suit. His timing had been exquisite—for him. For Endicott Tech, it had been a nightmare. By the time we'd settled, I'd just wanted to get Phillip out of my life.

"We don't just invest in companies, Noah," Maggie said, leaning forward, her blue eyes fixed on mine. "We invest in people. So far, we like you. We're inclined to give you the benefit of the doubt where the accusations of theft are concerned. You work hard, and you seem to care about your employees. That says something. We care about our employees, too. Do you think we would let Ella take care of our daughter if she wasn't important to us?"

"I don't know you well enough to say," I hedged.

"Cut the bullshit, man," Vance said. "Ella's been with us for a while. She's like family. So tell me, when you approached us about investing, did you know Ella worked for us?"

Shit. This was it. I had to decide if I was going to cut the line and walk or come clean and see what happened.

I couldn't afford to walk.

"I knew she worked for you," I said. "Not when I started researching you. You were at the top of my list before I had any idea that Ella would be involved. I came to you because I wanted to work with someone who saw more than just a balance sheet. You're right, my employees are important to me, and I don't want anyone involved in my company who can't respect that. You have a reputation that led me to think we could work together."

"When did you find out that Ella worked for us?" Maggie asked.

"About a month ago. It wasn't relevant. I'd been planning on coming back to Atlanta to see her anyway. To be honest, this would be less complicated if she didn't work for you. A lot less complicated."

That was the understatement of the century. When my investigation had turned up Ella's name in connection with Vance and Maggie Winters, my heart had leaped in anticipation before plummeting into my gut. Winning back Ella would be a challenge. Mixing up our relationship with my business was the last thing I needed.

"What happened to your nose?" Vance asked, one eyebrow raised in speculation.

"She punched me," I admitted. I'd been honest so far. No point in changing that now.

"What did you do?" Maggie asked, her eyes narrowed in disapproval. Vance smirked at me, his gaze knowing and amused.

"I can guess," he said. "Looks like she didn't appreciate your attempt at reconciliation."

"Look, Ella asked me to keep whatever happened between us private. I promised her that I would. It isn't your business. I'm glad you care about her. But if she wants to tell you what happened, that's up to her."

"Even if I say the deal is off unless you talk?" Vance tested.

"Do you want to do business with me if I'm capable of making a promise and then turning around and breaking it?" I asked.

"If she's not okay, we're going to have a problem," Vance said. "But for now, I'll drop it. Take a seat, and we'll run through this one more time before we wrap it up."

I sat, and we lost ourselves in numbers, graphs, and my plans for our new technology. Vance was right. If our software could disable a drone without interfering with local

Wi-Fi signals—which would be breaking the law—everyone would want to get their hands on it. There were other companies chasing the same goal. As far as I knew, we were at the head of the pack, but if we ran out of money, we wouldn't be for long.

I tried to focus on our meeting. When I'd flown out here from California, saving my company had been my number one priority. We were so close to a huge breakthrough, and I'd sunk every penny the company had into development. If I didn't get an influx of cash to tide us over, everything I'd worked for over the past two years would fall apart.

Nothing was more important than Endicott Tech.

Nothing except Ella.

I'd been telling Vance and Maggie the truth. For more than a year, I'd been thinking about Ella. Missing her. Wishing I'd never let her go. I'd wanted to come back for her long before this, but business always seemed to get in the way. Business and my own fears. When I realized Vance and Magnolia Winters were located in Atlanta, it seemed like fate. Still, Endicott Tech had been at the top of my mind.

It had to stay there. This wasn't just about me, about my ambitions and my dreams. I had fifteen people working for me. People with families and mortgages. People who had left stable jobs with benefits, seduced by the chance of a big payday and convinced by my larger-than-life public persona.

Maybe it doesn't say much about human nature, but when you're on the covers of business and tech magazines right and left, and everyone is shouting that you're the next big thing, people tend to have confidence in you. The publicity was superficial shit. Superficial, but it got me top-tier programmers.

A few had jumped ship during the lawsuit, but most of them had stuck with me. I owed them. They'd devoted their careers to me. Now, I had to deliver. I couldn't let them down. And after everything I'd sacrificed to get this company started, Ella most of all, I couldn't fail now.

All of that was true. And yet, the details of my business struggled to keep my attention, warring with the memory of kissing Ella. I could still feel her soft lips, her fingers burying themselves in my hair, the slick heat of her on my finger. With a willpower I didn't think I possessed, I forced my attention back on the meeting and managed to keep it together long enough to wrap things up.

When we were done, I gathered my papers together and stood. Vance stood with me and said, "We need some more time to go through this. Why don't we plan to get together later in the week or Monday? What's your timeframe for getting back to California?"

"Flexible, for the moment," I answered. That was accurate enough. I'd initially planned to stay only a few days, but now that I'd laid eyes on Ella, I wasn't leaving until we'd settled things between us.

"We'll be in touch," Vance said.

He didn't mention Ella again. He didn't need to. His warning had been clear.

I drove back to the Four Seasons in Midtown on autopilot. It had been a few years, but I still knew Atlanta like the back of my hand. When I'd lived here before, I'd been a struggling student in a shitty apartment, surviving on a diet of cheap food and highly caffeinated sodas. My first few months in California were the same, but worse. Rent in California was insane compared to Atlanta.

Then, overnight, everything changed. Four months after I left school and founded Endicott Tech, I licensed the first version of my drone software to the military, and money poured from the sky. I'd already started on the software we were working on now, and I was able to hire more programmers for my team.

Drones are hot, and the media jumped on my tech, making me into some kind of poster boy for the new wave of young Silicon Valley billionaires. Forget that I wasn't a billionaire. Nobody cared about that.

I was young and smart, and thanks to Ella's loving guidance in college, I had enough style that I looked good on the cover of a magazine. For a while, especially after Ella and I split up, I went crazy, dating models and B-movie actresses, buying an expensive house and a sports car. I was all about the flash.

Anything to help me forget that I didn't have Ella anymore.

When Philip's lawsuit hit and I went from golden boy to villain overnight, the acclaim dried up. It was a valuable lesson. Superficial shit was just that—superficial. It meant nothing.

The only things in my life that mattered were my company and Ella. And right now, I only had one of them.

If I couldn't talk Vance and Maggie into investing, I'd have nothing.

I'd like to think I'd learned from the past.

Okay, I was at the Four Seasons, and I was in a suite. But it was a junior suite, not the expansive corner suite I might've gotten a year or two ago. I needed the space, especially if I was going to be in town more than a few days. I had work to do, and I wasn't piling on my bed with my laptop. I wasn't a student anymore.

Yes, I was hoping the hotel and the suite would impress Ella. The thing is, I had money. I had more money than any twenty-five-year-old should. Plenty of money to spend on hotel suites, more than enough to impress my girl. So why didn't I just invest in my company myself?

I had. I hadn't taken a salary in a year and a half. Not since we'd diverted almost all of our programmers from smaller, profitable projects into the one we all knew would be our big payday. It was a risk, and since I was the one with enough in the bank to live on, I stopped taking a salary.

I could've poured my personal bank accounts into Endicott Tech. I would, if it came to that. I'm smart, and even under the cloud of Phillip's accusations, my reputation meant I could find work. If Endicott Tech went under, I wouldn't starve. None of my people would. They're the best.

But I'd promised them success beyond their wildest dreams, and I was going to fucking make good on that promise. Without draining my savings account and selling my house.

I let myself into the suite and kicked my shoes off, dropping my messenger bag on the desk and throwing myself on the couch. I had to get my head in gear.

I'd come to Atlanta for two things—business and Ella. I'd done all I could on the business front, for now. Vance and Maggie would do their thing over the next few days. When they were ready for a second meeting, they'd call. For now, all of my attention was on Ella.

What the fuck was she doing nannying? She liked kids, loved working with them in STEM classes, and got all fired up when she got one of them to fall in love with coding like she had when she was young. But babysitting? That was a massive waste of her time.

Ella was fucking smart as hell. I'd always loved her brain, the way she could fall into music, play her violin like she was bleeding her soul into the strings, and then turn around and take all of that passion and throw it into coding —so logical and precise but in her hands, alive.

All she'd wanted two years ago was to get her master's at Georgia Tech. Oliver Johnstone had promised her a spot in his project, and she'd wanted that more than anything. More than she'd wanted me. So why wasn't she doing it? What had happened?

I hated that there was no one I could ask.

Ella and I had shared the same friends, and when we'd split, most of them had taken her side, not that they were still in Atlanta. But those who'd remained had made it clear that they were Team Ella all the way. I was the asshole who'd ditched them for the glitter of Silicon Valley.

Then Phillip had accused me of stealing the code I'd used for my first drone project, and the rest of my friends had dropped off the face of the earth. At least as far as I was concerned. That was fine. I didn't need friends who'd walk away the second life got tough.

But Ella . . . getting the text after I missed her graduation had been painful, but I'd seen it coming. When she'd called me after the news broke on the lawsuit, I should have realized it was my chance to get her back. Instead, I'd wasted it and ended up driving her off for good.

I hadn't understood how much I needed her.

The thing is, I was still pissed at her. The breakup hadn't been all my fault. Yes, I was obsessed with my company. And yes, I should've paid more attention to my girlfriend. But she never got that I wasn't just doing this for me. I didn't care about the accolades and the attention . . . not until I didn't have Ella anymore.

When we were still together, everything was about us. About our future. Ella's field was never going to be a magnet for big money. She'd probably spend most of her career writing endless grant requests and hoping her projects could get funding. But if I could make my dreams come true, I could fund hers without a second thought.

To her credit, Ella never gave a shit about money. She'd been more excited about the software I'd developed than she had about the check I got when I sold it. And maybe I didn't explain myself as well as I could have, but for fuck's sake, I was twenty-three. She could've had a little patience.

I propped my feet up on the couch cushions and scrubbed the heels of my hands against my eyes. I'd taken the red-eye in, and I was fucking exhausted. My nose hurt from Ella's well-aimed punch. And I was starving.

I called room service and ordered a burger and a beer. One problem easily solved. I was going to eat, check in on work, and pass out early. Tomorrow, I was going to find out where Ella was living. I needed to get her to talk to me. I refused to believe we were over.

Not after that kiss.

She was mad enough to punch me. Ella didn't have much of a temper. If she'd punched me, she had to be really fucking pissed. But the second my mouth had hit hers, she'd melted.

Having her in my arms again was like coming home.

Ella was my first. Jesus, I was lucky she'd already been in love with me the first time we'd had sex because I'd lasted about thirty seconds. Fucking embarrassing. Fortunately, I'd had enough presence of mind to make sure she got hers first.

I'd been head over heels in love with her, and by the time we finally did the deed, I'd had my hands and mouth all over her luscious body. It could've been a disaster, but with Ella, everything had always been easy.

We'd laughed in bed as much as we did out of it, never

afraid to experiment, to learn each other's bodies. Together, we could do anything, or so I'd always thought. Once we'd figured sex out, it seemed like we fucked nonstop.

No one could blow my mind like Ella.

She probably thought I'd slept my way through Northern California. She'd be wrong. I'm not going to say there hadn't been other women. There were. Especially right after we split. It didn't take me more than a few months to realize that empty sex with faceless women would never be anywhere close to being with Ella.

I tried finding another girlfriend and had even dated a woman for a few months. When I'd realized that even a smart, funny, sexy woman paled in comparison to the memory of my first love, I'd broken it off and buried myself in work.

Fatigue dragged at me. By the time I finished eating, I wouldn't be good for much. I rolled off the couch and snagged my laptop out of the bag on the desk. Settling back in against the cushions, I flipped it open and stared at the screen.

Decisions, decisions.

My email demanded attention.

But I still didn't know where Ella was.

So far, I'd held off spying on her, not wanting to be a creep. But I couldn't ask Vance or Maggie where she lived, and I'd been blocked on her phone for two years. Blocked, but not completely locked out.

Giving in to my baser instincts, I pulled up an app that could track the GPS on her phone, assuming she hadn't gotten a new one. The app fired up and found her in seconds. My chest tightened in anticipation when I saw that she was only a few blocks away, somewhere in midtown.

I looked up the address, expecting to find an apartment

building. It was hard to determine exactly what it was. There was no commercial listing for the address, and it wasn't an apartment. I left the app open, programming it to tell me if her signal moved, and opened my email. There wasn't anything I could do about Ella at the moment, and my company needed me.

Once I had a chance to get some food and a good night's sleep, I was going after my girl.

This time, I wasn't going to let her walk away.

Chapter Four
Noah

My plan to track down Ella went sideways twenty minutes after I woke up. First thing in the morning, her signal was still at the mystery address in midtown, but shortly after that, it started to move, heading straight toward Buckhead. She was on her way to work at Vance and Magnolia's house. As much as I wanted to see Ella, I wasn't stupid enough to pursue her there. Acting like a creepy stalker was not the way to win over my potential investors.

It wasn't like I didn't have plenty to keep me busy. I hit the hotel gym, worked out, and went for a run. The rest of the day, I spent at the desk in my suite, surrounded by the detritus of two room service meals and endless cups of black coffee.

My team had made a breakthrough while I'd been sleeping the night before, but as it so often happened, the breakthrough came with bugs. We were all racing to sort them out and see if our progress would stick. It was killing me to be this close to a viable product, this close to more money than any of us had ever seen in our lifetimes, and yet miles away if we couldn't untangle the code.

I finally lifted my head from my laptop when my stomach growled. My brain was on West Coast time as I worked in sync with my team, but my stomach hadn't been filled since noon.

I checked the clock.

4:30 PM.

Ella's signal was moving very slowly. Too slowly for a car. She was either walking or jogging. She was in a popular nearby park, probably out for a run.

I kept an eye on her progress as I changed and splashed water on my face. I thought about getting something to eat but decided to wait and see if I could talk Ella into dinner. When her signal left the park and sped up, I headed down to get my rental car. Following a hunch, I drove to the mystery address in midtown, betting that's where she'd show up.

As I'd hoped, a few minutes after I parked on the street in front of the building, Ella's hatchback passed me, turning into the alley beside the building. I got out of my car and followed her, moving just fast enough to see her car disappear into a garage.

Dammit.

I strode back to the front, planning to ring the bell when she yanked the door open and glared at me.

Her cheeks were flushed, and stray curls of dark hair stuck to her damp skin. I'd been right—she'd been jogging. I tried not to leer at her. Her clothes weren't revealing. She wore long, black, stretchy leggings and a loose, long-sleeve, wicking T-shirt over a jogging bra.

But I knew what was underneath. I knew her body as

well as I knew my own. My hands had been all over her the day before, and it hadn't been nearly enough.

"What are you doing here?" she demanded. "How did you find me? I know Vance and Magnolia didn't tell you where I was."

"I tracked you down," I said unapologetically. "What is this place? It looks commercial. Do you live here now?"

The building was a nondescript brick square from the outside, taking up all of a short block, surrounded by commercial properties. There were no windows on the first floor that could be seen from the street, though the second floor had tall multi-paned windows that gleamed in the afternoon sun. It looked like a body shop or a warehouse, not a home.

Realizing she wasn't going to get rid of me that easily, Ella let out a breath of defeat and said, "Vance used to live here. He and Maggie can't decide what to do with it, and I didn't have a place, so they offered it to me temporarily."

"That was nice of them," I said inanely, my mind racing. Why didn't Ella have a place to live?

"Noah, what do you want?"

"I want to talk to you."

"We have nothing to talk about."

"I disagree. Look, just give me a little time. An hour or two. Come get dinner with me. If you really don't want to see me after that, I'll leave you alone."

Ella stared at me. My heart pounded in my chest, every nerve in my body on edge as I waited. Finally, after what felt like a lifetime, she said, "Come in. I'm not having dinner with you. I have plans. You can wait while I get changed, and I'll have a coffee with you on the way. There's a place down the street. But that's it."

I followed her in, my eyes glued to the roll of her hips as

she stalked down the hall to a freight elevator. She didn't say a word as we rode up a flight to the second floor of the building. The elevator door opened into a modern, luxurious loft.

I didn't have any trouble imagining Vance Winters living in the space, though I could see why he and Magnolia had moved to their far bigger house in Buckhead.

The loft was ultra-cool with soaring ceilings, exposed beams, and modern finishes. But it was also a completely open plan which I could imagine would be a nightmare with a baby in the house, especially when your home also served as an office and an artist's studio.

Ella pointed to the stools at the kitchen island and ordered, "Wait there," before disappearing down the hall to the right. A minute later, I heard the shower turn on.

Typical of Ella, it didn't take her long to get ready. She emerged from the hallway twenty minutes later, her long, dark hair wet and pulled up into a sloppy bun, wearing faded skinny jeans. Her flowing, gauzy shirt draped over her body in shades of red, revealing her curves without flaunting them.

I'd always loved the way Ella dressed. She had her share of T-shirts and hoodies, but she usually favored things like this—light fabrics and bright colors in whimsical designs. Her artistic side came out in her sense of fashion, and she knew what flattered her. Ella had an effortless beauty that no overly made-up model or actress could hope to match.

I shoved my hands in my pockets to keep from reaching for her.

"You ready to go?" I asked. She gave a short nod and picked up her purse and keys off the counter.

"You can follow me in your car. There's parking there."

"Why don't I ride with you?" I asked, not liking how this was going.

"Because I'm not coming back here afterward, and I don't want to give you a ride anywhere."

"I'll follow you," I conceded. I'd known getting back into Ella's good graces would be hard, but this was worse than expected.

She led the way in silence, and I left her at the front door to get my car. Our destination wasn't far, a tall, historic-looking building, also in midtown, that appeared to be a combination of residential apartments, businesses, and small retail properties. We parked in an aboveground lot behind the building, and Ella led me through the rear entrance to the first-floor atrium, which had a coffee shop, an art gallery, and a few other stores. I caught sight of a plaque that read *Winters House*.

The Winters family again. How did Ella get so wrapped up in their business? Too many questions, and no answers.

At the door to the coffee shop, I looked at Ella and asked, "Chai tea latte?"

Her eyes flared in surprise before narrowing. She jerked one shoulder in a half-shrug and said, "Please. I'll get us a table."

The café had a soup and sandwich menu, as well as a case of mouthwatering pastries. I was hungry, but real food would have to wait. Maybe there was still a chance to convince Ella to eat dinner with me. Out of the corner of my eye, I watched her get a table for two by the front window and studiously stare out into the street, avoiding looking at me.

Fuck, she was pissed.

Two years later, and she could barely stand the sight of me. That had to mean something. If she didn't care, then this would just be like two old friends getting together.

Instead, she'd alternated between anger and falling apart in my arms. I had to take this is a good sign. I refused to admit that my quest to win her back might fail.

I ordered our drinks—her chai latte and my Americano —and a chocolate croissant. Ella had always loved chocolate croissants. When she saw the pastry, her eyes did that little flare again. Did she think I'd forgotten her favorite foods? I hadn't forgotten anything.

I remembered it all—what she liked to eat, her favorite bands, and the way she liked to be kissed. How to fuck her so she'd come fast, and how to tease her until she begged. I remembered it all, and I wanted all of it back.

"Okay, we're here, Noah. What do you want?"

Time to lay it all out on the table.

"I miss you," I said. "I miss you, and I want to try again."

"No, you don't." Ella stared down at the croissant, her long fingers picking at the pastry. "I haven't heard from you in two years, Noah. Not since we broke up. Now you see me once, and all of a sudden, you decide you want me back? No. Just, no."

"You think seeing you yesterday was an accident?" I asked. "You think I just stumbled across you and all of a sudden changed my mind about our breakup?"

"That's what it looks like," she said flatly.

"You're wrong," I said. "There was nothing accidental about yesterday. I didn't know you would be at the meeting, but I knew you worked for Vance and Maggie and I planned to track you down while I was here. Hell, part of the reason I picked them was to give me an excuse to be in Atlanta."

Ella took a tiny sip of her latte, swallowed, and tilted her head to the side. "So, you wanted to see me, but you couldn't make time in your schedule until business brought you here."

Shit. When she put it like that, it sounded bad. Explanations about the kind of pressure I was under and everything that was going on with the company were not going to make my case.

Shit.

Sometimes, the best defense is a good offense.

"Why are you working as a nanny? Why aren't you working in your field? Or in school? Shouldn't you have graduated in May?"

Ella's face closed down. Just like that, the vitality drained from her dark eyes, her shoulders went stiff, and she turned her face away.

"That's none of your business."

"Why won't you tell me? What happened?" I demanded.

Ella crossed her arms over her chest and raised her chin. "I don't have to explain my life to you. Not anymore. I'm not your business. We're not getting back together, okay? Even if I wanted to, I don't have room in my life right now—"

She cut off abruptly. I shifted from curious to alarmed. What the fuck was going on? My Ella was driven, determined, and completely focused on her academic career. Hell, she'd sacrificed our relationship for school and her future. It was that important to her, and now she'd left it behind?

I wasn't walking away without an answer.

"Ella, tell me what's going on. Tell me now, or I'll start digging, and I'll find the truth. You know I will. Why don't you make it easy and just tell me?"

Her chin dropped, and she let out a breath. Yeah, she knew when I had her beaten. I wasn't a hacker, but with a little work, I could find out what I needed to know. More importantly, I knew people who could get every detail of her life way faster than I could on my own. I didn't want to invade her privacy that way, but I would. And she knew it.

"I had to drop out of school, okay?"

"Why?"

"I couldn't afford it anymore. My dad lost his job, and he didn't tell anyone, just kept borrowing money, and then it all fell apart, and there wasn't anything left."

"But you had grants, and you were working," I said, feeling sick at the thought of what she must've gone through. I'd worked my way through school too. It was one of the things we'd had in common.

"I did, but they weren't enough without my parents' help. I tried getting a loan, but it's too much. I don't want to borrow money. I don't want to end up like my dad, buried under debt without any options. I'm not like you. I can't design some software that'll make me billions of dollars."

"I don't have billions of dollars," I said under my breath. You get one windfall in Silicon Valley, and everyone starts throwing around the term 'tech billionaire.' Ella snorted in derision.

"Close enough," she said.

"Then why didn't you ask me for help? You could've called me. You know I would have—"

"Are you fucking kidding me?" she demanded in a shout that had half of the coffee shop turning to stare. Ella flushed and lowered her voice, but her dark eyes glowed with rage. "You dumped me. You didn't even bother to come home for my college graduation. I told you I didn't want to see you anymore, and you never got in touch with me again. The next thing I know, you've got a new girl on your arm every week, going to movie premieres and being interviewed on TV, and you think I'd call you and ask you for money?"

"You could have," I said quietly. "You could've asked me for anything."

Her eyes hardened, and she shook her head. "How could you expect me to think that's true? You walked away from me and never looked back."

"Ella, that's not what happened."

"Bullshit, that isn't what happened. That's exactly what happened. And I don't need your help. I'm working. I'm saving money. I'm going back to school, and I *will* graduate. It's just going to take a little more time. I don't need your charity, and I don't need you to feel sorry for me."

"I don't feel sorry for you," I said automatically. We both knew I was lying.

How could I *not* feel sorry for her?

I'd never known anyone who loved academics as much as Ella. We'd both been good students, but half the time, I'd been restless, plans for the future rolling in my head, driving me to do more than study and get good grades. For most students, a free ride to a grad program at Caltech was like winning the lottery, but I hadn't lasted more than a semester. I'd wanted to be out there, building my company and making things happen.

I wasn't going to change the world from inside a class-room. Not like Ella was.

"I'm sorry," I said. "How are your parents doing?"

I hadn't been particularly close with Ella's family, but we'd had an amicable relationship. Her parents were nice people, if a little obsessed with status. I couldn't imagine they were handling the change in their circumstances very well.

Ella broke off a piece of croissant and took a bite. After

she'd swallowed, she said, "They're okay. My dad finally got another job. They're living in a condo, and my mom is looking for something, but, you know, she never worked, so there's not a lot out there."

"How did you get hooked up with Vance and Maggie?" I asked. It seemed so random. I'd never known Ella to so much as babysit for extra cash, and now she was a full-time nanny?

"I got to be friends with these two girls in my old building before I had to drop out. Jo and Emily. They were in the CS program too. We hung out a lot, even after I left school. I lost my apartment, and I was couch surfing with some other friends, waiting tables—"

"You hated waiting tables," I said quietly. A husky half-laugh erupted from Ella's throat before she snapped her mouth shut and cut off the sound.

"Yeah, well, I also suck at it. Jo and Emily started dating Holden and Tate Winters—it was so weird. In like two weeks, they went from single to joined at the hip, both of them. Which is cool, because Holden and Tate are both good guys, perfect for Jo and Emily. But they knew I was in a tight spot, so they started giving me some freelance coding work—they own WGC. And then when Vance and Maggie got together, and they needed a nanny, Jo and Emily knew I liked kids, so they recommended me. I was lucky. They're great to work for, and with Vance letting me stay in his loft, I don't have to spend money on rent so I can save more for school and living expenses when I go back."

"That *was* lucky," I agreed.

I understood why Ella hadn't called me for help. I did. I hadn't gone out of my way to be accessible after we broke up. Still, it burned knowing that virtual strangers had stepped in to see that she had work and shelter while I'd done nothing. That I hadn't known what was going on didn't feel like much of an excuse.

"I'm sorry you had to drop out of school," I said.

"Me too. So, why are you talking to Vance and Maggie about your company?" she asked, obviously trying to change the subject.

I thought about what to say. My ego told me to feed her a line of bullshit about growing the company. My heart warned me that lies were not the way to go.

"About a year ago," I explained, "I changed the tack of the company. We'd been working on some small navigation-related apps that were profitable but boring. In the mean-time, we'd been working on our current project, and when it started to take off, I made the decision to divert resources to development. I was betting we could make the new program work before we ran out of money."

"But it's not done, and you're running out of money?" Ella asked, one eyebrow raised.

"Exactly. We're close. No more than a few months away, even by a conservative estimate. But between now and then, I need to keep the lights on and pay my people."

"So you're broke?" Ella asked.

"Not exactly. Personally, I'm doing just fine."

Ella's dark eyebrows knit together. "Then why don't you just invest your own money? Why come to Vance and Maggie?"

"I will. If I have to. But it's not good business. If I gamble my savings on keeping the company afloat and I lose, I've got nothing left to start over. Besides, we have a viable prod-uct. We're a good bet for investors. I'm not here because Maggie and Vance were my only option. I'm here because they're offering me the best deal and I'd prefer to work with them."

"And if you didn't need the money? Would you still have come back here?"

This conversation was littered with pitfalls.

Honesty, I reminded myself. *Be honest.*

"Yes," I said. "I told you, I'm not just here to see Vance and Maggie. I'm here to see you. If I didn't have this meeting with Vance and Maggie, I don't know that I'd be here right now. My team needs me back in California. But that doesn't mean I haven't been thinking about you. I wanted to wait until things were calmer with the company. Until I could focus on you. The timing isn't good right now, but I'm here, and I want to try."

Ella shrugged her shoulder and took another bite of the croissant, her eyes fixed on the view of the street out the window. I didn't want to lie to her, but my honesty didn't seem to be winning me any points.

"Look, Ella, I know I didn't handle things well when we split up. I know I was self-centered and an asshole. By the time I realized I'd fucked up and I wanted you back, I couldn't figure out how to fix everything that had gone wrong. I've been dragging my feet, but it's not because you aren't a priority. It's because getting you back means more than anything else, and I didn't want to fuck it up again, so it was easier just to keep putting it off."

Ella let out a gust of breath. Her phone beeped, and she checked the screen. She typed out a quick text and said, "There's a part of me that wants to believe you, Noah. When we broke up—" she halted and bit her lip, staring at the ceiling as her eyes filled with tears.

Fuck.

Fuck. If Ella started crying, I was gonna lose it. Guilt, cold, sticky, and heavy, settled in my gut. Our breakup wasn't all my fault, but that didn't make me feel any better about the pain in her eyes.

She blinked rapidly, washing away the tears, and stood. "I have to go. I have plans. I was supposed to be there half an hour ago."

"Go out with me tomorrow."

"I don't know. I have to think. I don't know. I'll call you."

Ella snatched her purse and keys off the table and rushed out, leaving her drink and the croissant behind.

I got up to follow her, but when I hit the lobby, she'd disappeared.

CHAPTER FIVE
ELLA

I'd never been more grateful that I was a frequent visitor at Winters House. Security checked me through quickly and waved me off to the residential elevator bank. I couldn't handle another second with Noah.

I wanted to believe him. I wanted to believe that he really had missed me. That he regretted the way things had ended. I just couldn't. He'd cut me out of his life and moved on. He said he wasn't back just because Vance and Maggie were here, but how could I know if that was true? The reality was that Noah hadn't bothered to come back until it was for his company.

He could sit at his desk in California thinking fond thoughts of me, but he hadn't actually *done* anything about it until money was on the line.

I'd been shattered when he'd dumped me the first time. Out of school, my life in limbo, everything felt too fragile to risk another broken heart.

I rode the elevator up to the floor where Holden and Tate lived. They each had an apartment that spanned half the building—a perk of being a Winters—though based on what they'd said about Holden's older brother Jacob, who owned the building, I had no doubt they'd paid full price before Jacob let them move in.

Tate's door swung open as I stepped out of the elevator. Jo leaned out, her long, streaky, blonde hair swinging into the hall.

"Hey, where have you been? We were starting to get worried."

"Sorry. I'll tell you in a minute, but first, I need a drink."

"Sure, we've got a bottle of wine open—"

I walked into the apartment and said, "No, not a glass of wine. I need a drink. Like tequila. Or vodka."

"Okay, now I *am* worried. What happened? Did Oliver give you bad news?"

"Yes, but that's not it. I wasn't expecting him to be able to get me back in anyway. It just sucked to hear it."

"So what happened?"

I followed Jo into the kitchen to see Emily leaning against the counter, pressed into Tate's side, his arm wrapped tightly around her shoulder. I'd gotten used to seeing the two of them like that. When they were within arm's reach, Tate always had her tucked in close, as if he'd protect her from anything. I'm pretty sure that was his life's plan. Keep Emily safe and happy.

I didn't know anyone who deserved it more. Her gray eyes lit with concern as Jo's words registered and she asked, "Did something happen? You look terrible."

"Em," Tate said in a chiding voice that was half laugh. Looking at me, he shook his head and said, "You don't look terrible. You look gorgeous, as always. But you do look shell-shocked. What's going on?"

"Alcohol first," I said, jumping up to sit on the counter across from the island. Holden, Jo's boyfriend and Tate's cousin, was at the stove stirring some kind of sauce. A steaming pot of water bubbled on a back burner. I caught sight of a baking sheet covered with Emily's signature bruschetta. Sweet. I had a feeling pasta would be just the thing to soak up the tequila shots I had in mind.

Anything to numb my reaction to seeing Noah.

"So what's going on?" Jo asked.

"I know what's going on," Holden said, his dark eyes warm with concern. To me, he said, "Let me guess—the Noah Endicott who's been talking to Vance and Maggie about investing is the same Noah you broke up with a few months before you met Jo and Em."

I pointed a finger at Holden and said, "Bingo."

"What?" Jo asked from the living room where she was raiding the makeshift liquor cabinet to get me a drink. She came back carrying two bottles, one a lemon-flavored vodka and the other a cinnamon schnapps with gold flakes swirling lazily in the clear liquid. I knew from experience that I'd hate myself tomorrow if I drank the cinnamon schnapps, but there was no way I was touching lemon-flavored anything.

After kissing Noah and remembering the way he always tasted of lemon and mint, lemons were out.

"You have a terrible liquor selection," she complained to Tate. He laughed and gave a shrug.

"We own a nightclub. If we want to drink liquor, we go to Mana. I didn't even know I had that stuff."

I pointed at the bottle of schnapps and said, "That one."

"Have you seen him? Did you talk to him?" Jo asked, finding a juice glass and pouring a healthy measure of the cinnamon schnapps inside. She handed it to me, watching with concern as I threw it back. The sweet fire burned my throat. I coughed twice and swallowed hard before I answered.

"I interrupted their meeting yesterday," I said. "I had no idea he was coming, and I've never said anything about him to Vance or Maggie, so they had no reason to think they should mention it to me. I just walked in, and there he was."

"What did he do when he saw you?" Emily asked. She extracted herself from Tate's hold to slide the bruschetta in the oven.

In answer, I held out my juice glass. Jo refilled it for me, but not without giving me the side-eye. "I'm not going to stop you, but watch out. You don't drink that much, and you haven't eaten yet. You'll make yourself sick."

I emptied the glass, sputtering a little. Already, warmth had spread through my chest, dulling the ache from seeing Noah. I wasn't going to drink much more. Emily was right. I'd regret it later.

"So? What did he say when he saw you?" Holden asked.

"How did you know he was here?" Jo broke in.

"Vance asked me a few weeks ago if I knew anything about Endicott Tech, aside from the obvious. It's harder to do research when that lawsuit dominates their press. It's not really our area, but I remembered the name, and I made a few calls. I had no idea he had an appointment with Vance yesterday, or I would have said something."

I set the juice glass on the counter beside me. "It's okay. He knew I would be there. At least he knew I worked for them. He says he didn't just come here for business. He says he came back for me."

"What do you think?" Tate asked.

"I don't know. I don't know what I think. I thought I

hated him. I thought I was over him. And then he kissed me and—"

"What?" Emily shouted, interrupting me. "When did he kiss you? Tell me he didn't kiss you in the middle of the meeting."

I shook my head. "No. I ran out like the great big baby I am, and he followed me into the kitchen while I was trying to find my keys. We started fighting, and then he kissed me."

"Was it good?" Jo asked in a low voice.

I nodded.

"Really good?" She asked.

I nodded again.

Thinking about it, I said, "You know how sometimes you and Holden start kissing and then the next thing you know, the rest of us have to leave the room because we think you two are about to start going at it right in front of us?"

Emily and Tate busted out laughing. They knew what I was talking about. Anyone who'd been in the same room with Holden and Jo for longer than twenty minutes knew what I was talking about. Those two weren't capable of keeping their hands off each other, and once they got going . . .

Shooting a heated look at Jo, Holden said, "That good, huh?"

"Hey, I've been doing just fine on my own," I protested. "I really thought I was completely over him. Then one kiss, and I would've let him strip me naked in the middle of the kitchen. My bosses' kitchen! I have to stay away from him."

"What if you don't?" Emily asked quietly. We all stared at her as if she'd suddenly grown horns on her forehead. "I'm just saying. You haven't dated anyone seriously since you broke up with Noah. Have you even slept with anyone?"

"Emily!" This was embarrassing, especially in the

company of two happy couples who I was sure had sex multiple times a day. Emily's eyes narrowed on mine. Emily was one of the most thoughtful, sweet, and considerate people I knew. She was also very conscious of respecting other people's comfort zones. Considering she'd been dealing with a severe anxiety disorder for most of her life, she was usually the last person to push anyone where they didn't want to go. If she was pushing me, she must think she had a good reason.

"Hey," she said, "the four of us are your best friends. If you can't talk about sex with us . . . so be honest. Have you even hooked up with anyone since Noah?"

"I went out with that guy from school a while ago. He kissed me at my door when he dropped me off," I offered.

Jo let out a snort of laughter. "Ella, that was more than six months ago, and you said it was a terrible kiss. Doesn't count."

"So there hasn't been anyone since this Noah guy?" Tate asked, reaching out to snag Emily's hand and pull her back into his side. He dropped an almost absent kiss on the top of her head before tightening his arm around her waist.

I was going to need another drink if this was where the conversation was going. Trying to ignore the heat in my cheeks, I admitted, "Basically, no. There hasn't been anyone since Noah. And there wasn't anyone before Noah. There's just been Noah."

"And we all know what Noah's been up to since you broke up," Jo said under her breath.

"Exactly," I said. "He dumped me, and a week later, he was all over the Internet at some Tech conference with a sleazy model on his arm."

"And she was just the first," Jo said. "If rumors are true,

he's slept his way through half of California in the last two years."

"When he wasn't being sued for stealing the code he used to found his company," Tate cut in. "I don't like this guy hanging around you, Ella."

"I don't know much about the lawsuit," Jo said, "but I do know he's a manwhore. Anyone with access to the internet knows that."

Holden elbowed her in the side, and she glared at him. "What? It's true. He's like the poster boy for tech-billionaire player."

Holden cleared his throat and said, "Because the media always tells the truth, right?"

Jo sent me an apologetic look and turned to finish up the pasta. She and I were the only people in this room who didn't have good reason to hate and distrust the media. The entire Winters family had grown up with their lives under a microscope. Tate's parents had died in a grisly murder-suicide when he'd been a child. Combined with their wealth and power, the scandal had been enough to draw unrelenting attention from the press.

When Holden's parents had been murdered years later in an almost identical crime, the media had been a nightmare. And Emily had almost broken up with Tate over the media's obsession with the Winters family. Her anxiety disorder started when she was a child and survived a mass-shooting. The press had hounded her so savagely she'd been afraid to leave the house and had ended up severely agoraphobic.

She and Tate were still navigating their relationship, learning how to balance her condition with a family that was in the limelight more often than not. For Holden, Tate, and Emily, the gut reaction would always be to distrust what they saw splashed on the papers and online.

I got where they were coming from. I did. But I'd seen the pictures. I'd seen Noah walking down the red carpet with a tall, skinny model on his arm. I'd seen pictures taken at SXSW—Noah kissing a hot up-and-coming actress, a drink in his hand. And there'd been more. After the first six months, I tried not to look. Once the lawsuit hit, the quality of the girls had fallen, but they were still there, hanging all over Noah. He never looked like he was trying to fight them off.

For the last year, between leaving school and focusing on work, I'd done a decent job of ignoring Noah's existence, but that didn't erase the memories of seeing his active social life thoroughly documented after we'd broken up.

"Ella, I'm not making excuses for him," Holden went on. "I'm your friend, not his. I don't even know the guy, and if he's making you this miserable, I don't want to. But I feel like I have to point out that men deal with breakups differently than women do."

"He's got a point," Tate said. "I know it must have sucked seeing him out there with other women while you were at home feeling like shit. But that doesn't mean he just moved on. It doesn't mean he didn't care. If you're still hung up on him after two years, maybe you should give him a chance."

"No way," Emily said, defending me. "He doesn't deserve a second chance. He bailed on her, didn't even come home for her college graduation, walked away from her for his company, and after two years, he decides he wants her back? No way."

"Thank you," I said. I hopped down off the counter, intending to fill my juice glass with another shot or two of the cinnamon schnapps. Emily was the closest, and she stepped in front of me, cutting me off.

"Nope, food. It's time for dinner. If you still want to drink more after you eat, I'll pour. But if you keep drinking now, you'll end up not eating at all, and then you'll really be sick tomorrow."

I let Emily herd me out of the kitchen and into the dining room, the others coming behind with serving plates laden with food. I was hungry. I hadn't been able to eat anything at the coffee shop with Noah, and lunch was a distant memory. I already had a vague headache forming behind my eyes, a side-effect of drinking the overly sweet alcohol on an empty stomach. The subject of Noah was dropped when we took our seats and portioned out plates of food.

The pasta was freshly made and covered in a light cream sauce with veggies and shrimp. I suddenly realized I was starving. I was chewing my first bite, rolling my eyes in pleasure, when Holden said quietly from across the table, "We don't have to talk about this anymore, but I just want to say that starting a company can be really distracting. I can't imagine trying to sustain a relationship during the first few years Tate and I were building WGC. Do you remember that?" he asked Tate.

Tate shook his head and wound pasta around his fork. "Shit, yeah. I slept on my couch in the office more nights than I made it home, and our office is only a few floors away. We worked pretty much around the clock. The stress was a killer."

Holden cut in, "God, it was. I only slept when I was completely exhausted. If I tried to close my eyes any other time, all I'd think about were numbers and deadlines and what would happen if the game didn't ship and what we would do if it didn't sell. Running the company is fun now, but those first few years it was a love-hate thing. More obsession than anything else."

"Are you going to see him again?" Emily asked.

"I don't think he's going to let me avoid him," I admitted. "I told him we had nothing to talk about, but he tracked me down at the loft this afternoon, and I had coffee with him. That's why I was late."

"If you can't get rid of him, I'll talk to Vance," Tate said. "If he's trying to convince Vance and Maggie to invest in Endicott Tech, he's not going to want to piss Vance off."

"Thanks, but Vance already talked to him," I said.

"So Vance and Maggie know about you and Noah?" Jo asked. I took a sip of wine and looked at the ceiling for a second before I answered.

"Well," I started, not sure how to explain, "after he kissed me, I kind of punched him. When I ran out, his nose was bleeding. Between that and the way I freaked when I saw him, Vance and Maggie knew something was up and I guess they dragged it out of him."

Both Holden and Tate gave a shout of laughter. Jo asked incredulously, "You punched him? You're, like, the least violent person I know."

"Yeah, well, the kiss got kind of . . . out of control. I was mad that he was back, and kind of embarrassed that I'd let it get that far, and he looked so smug I just . . ."

Tate had himself under control, but Holden was still laughing. "So he had to go back into a meeting with his investors with a bloody nose?" he asked.

I was starting to feel kind of bad about it. At the time, punching him had felt like vindication. After all the pain he'd put me through, he deserved a punch to the nose. Now that I knew what was on the line for his company, I was a lot less comfortable being in the middle of Noah's potential deal with Vance and Maggie.

"I need to apologize," I said mostly to myself. "Hitting him wasn't cool."

"He deserved it," Jo said loyally.

Maybe he did, but that didn't mean hitting him was okay. Dammit. I really was going to have to apologize.

"So Vance already talked to him? What did he say?" Tate asked.

"He didn't tell me, exactly," I said. "He just cornered me this morning when I came into work and told me to let him know if I was having any trouble with Noah and that he'd take care of it. He said he'd already told Noah that if I complained about him, the deal was off."

"Damn, Vance the hard ass. I would've expected that from Aidan or Jacob. Definitely from Gage. But Vance is usually chill," Tate said.

Holden sat back in his chair and picked up his wine, raising one eyebrow as he said, "True, but Genghis Khan would look laid-back next to Aidan, Jacob, or Gage. And since he got his shit together, Vance doesn't fuck around."

I only vaguely knew what Holden was talking about. I'd been working for Vance and Maggie since a few weeks after they got engaged, not long after Vance's surprise daughter, Rosalie, was dropped on his doorstep. I'd missed the drama of their courtship, though I'd heard bits and pieces from Jo and Emily. I'd also heard that before Rosie and Maggie, when Vance had still been with Rosie's mother, he'd had a drinking problem and was a functioning disaster.

I could barely imagine it. The Vance I knew definitely had his shit together.

"So how did coffee go?" Emily asked.

"We argued," I said. "He was pissed I didn't tell him

about school. He actually expected me to call him and ask for tuition money when I had to drop out. Can you believe that?" I was getting mad all over again.

Half under his breath, Tate said, "Bet that went well."

He and Holden had offered to lend me the money I needed to go back to school. I'd accepted the freelance work they sent my way but turned down the loan. If I was bothered by how long it was taking me to pay back an anonymous bank for a semester's worth of tuition, I couldn't begin to imagine the humiliation of owing a friend.

"Someday, you have to learn that it's okay to accept help from the people who care about you," Holden said gently.

"Yes, I know," I said tartly. "And the next time I need a ride home from the doctor's, I'll call one of you. And by the way, don't think I'm fooled by Vance letting me use his loft rent-free or you guys sending me work. He could rent that place out in a second for a ton of money. And there are a lot of other people more qualified to do the work you're giving me. So I *do* know how to accept help, and I appreciate it."

"Hey, if you weren't doing the job well, we wouldn't give you the work," Tate said.

"I know that. If I didn't think I could do it, I wouldn't accept it. And I appreciate it. I really, really do. I'm just saying there's a big difference between accepting a place to stay or some freelance work and accepting a check for a huge amount of money. I have at least another year left of school, and I need tuition and living expenses. That's a ton of cash. You guys are my friends, and it means a lot that you want to help. It does. Can we not talk about this anymore?"

"Yeah, fine, but what I want to know is, did you punch him again? While you were getting coffee? Because if you did, we might be able to get the video off the security cameras," Jo asked.

"No, I didn't punch him. I ran away again."

"What are you going to do the next time he tracks you down?" Emily asked.

"I have no idea," I said.

There had to be a compromise somewhere in the middle of punching him, kissing him, and running away.

I just hadn't found it yet.

CHAPTER SIX
ELLA

Tate and Emily drove me home. I didn't have any more of the cinnamon schnapps after dinner, but I'd had a glass of wine while I was eating and I was in no shape to get behind the wheel, even if I was only going a few blocks.

The jingle of my ringtone cut into the dark car as we pulled out of the parking lot. I checked it, curious. The number was unfamiliar. Normally, I'd let it ring through to voicemail, but I was just tipsy enough to answer.

"Hello?"

"Ella? Ella, it's Phillip. How are you? It's been a while."

"Phillip Martin?" I hadn't spoken to Phillip Martin in almost two years. Not since he'd sued Noah over the alleged stolen code. He'd called me once, right after the suit was filed, but I'd been so upset I'd hung up on him.

"Yeah. Long time no talk," he said in a jovial tone more suited to a conversation with a good friend, not an out of the blue call to someone he hadn't seen since college. Odd. "Listen, I heard that Noah was back in Atlanta and I just wanted to check in and make sure you're okay. Has he tried to see you?"

"Um, why are you asking, Phillip? Are you keeping tabs on him? Doesn't he have a restraining order against you?"

"That's old news," Phillip said, blowing off the restraining order and sidestepping my question. "No, we're going up for some of the same contracts, and I've been keeping an eye on him. When I heard he was going to be back in Atlanta, I was worried about you. I know you had a tough breakup."

Phillip's voice was heavy with sympathy, but something about it was off. My brain was mildly pickled on schnapps, but I knew enough to distrust Phillip Martin.

"We did," I said evenly. "But I'm fine now. Like you said. Old news."

"I heard you had a job with Vance Winters. Noah show up there?"

"Phillip, I'm sorry, but I have to go. My friends just showed to pick me up. It was nice talking to you. Take care."

I tapped the phone to hang up and stared down at the screen, the time of the call blinking at me.

What. The. Fuck?

"Did Phillip Martin just call you?" Emily asked in an incredulous voice. "I didn't think you knew him that well."

"I don't," I said slowly. "We were acquaintances in college, but that's it. He's never called me before. Except—"

"When did he call you before, Ella?" Tate asked, his voice low and dark. Belatedly, I noticed we were pulled over in the alley, not far from the parking lot behind his building.

"Right after he brought suit against Noah," I said. "I hung up on him, and he never called again."

"What did he want?" Emily asked, sounding worried.

"To make sure Noah wasn't bothering me. He knows I

work for Vance. He wanted to know if Noah had met with Vance."

"I don't like you in the middle of those two," Tate said. "That lawsuit got ugly before Noah settled. I'm not surprised Phillip Martin is watching Noah, but I don't like that he's watching you. How does he know you're working for Vance and Maggie?"

It was a good question.

"If he's watching Noah and found out he was talking to Vance, he might have looked into Vance. There was that picture last month," Emily pointed out.

I'd gone to the park with Vance and Maggie, playing with Rosie in the sun while my employers enjoyed a run together. Someone had snapped a picture of the happy family and caught me in the background. At the time, it hadn't seemed like a big deal. Now I wondered.

"He's going to try to mess up Noah's deal," I said, awareness dawning in my tipsy brain. "That's why he was checking to see if Noah met with Vance. That asshole."

"Maybe you should come back to our place," Emily said. "I don't like this guy watching you. Not with Noah trying to get to you, too."

"I thought you wanted me to give Noah a chance."

"I do, I think," Emily said hesitantly. "I want you to be happy. But this is getting weird. Whatever is going on with Phillip and Noah, you don't want to be in the middle."

"We've got plenty of room, Ella," Tate said. "So do Vance and Maggie."

"No," I said. "Vance has plenty of security on the loft. And Phillip is in California. He's not really interested in me anyway. He's all about Noah."

"And what about Noah?" Tate asked, pulling the car back into the street. "What are you going to do about him?"

"I don't know." I wasn't worried about being in the middle of Phillip and Noah. Their situation didn't have anything to do with me. I *was* worried about Phillip spying on Noah. Noah could take care of himself, but Phillip's fixation was unsettling.

We pulled up in front of Vance's building to see Noah leaning against the door.

Shit.

"Is that him?" Emily asked, her eyes wide. When I nodded, she said, "Damn, Ella, he's hot."

"I know," I said mournfully.

Though to be honest, when I looked at Noah, I didn't see what everyone else saw. I didn't see the hot young tech billionaire. I didn't see the notorious player. I just saw Noah.

Noah at nineteen with a bad haircut, still gangly, his dark eyes bright with intelligence and humor.

Noah at twenty-one, finally grown into his frame, his hair in a shaggy cut that made me swoon when the dark strands fell into his eyes.

Noah, naked beneath me in bed, his eyes wide with wonder and lust as I rode him.

I blinked hard and looked away.

"Do you want me to get rid of him?" Tate asked.

I shook my head. "I'm fine. You can just let me out here. I'll get my car tomorrow."

"I should at least have a word with him," Tate said, his voice hard as he pulled the car to a stop at the curb. "I don't like him just showing up here."

"It's okay, Tate," I promised. "Noah isn't dangerous."

"He is if he upsets you," Tate argued.

I leaned forward to squeeze his shoulder and said, "You're a good friend, Tate Winters. I'll be fine. I don't think he's going to leave me alone until I give him a chance to talk."

"I'll call you tomorrow," Emily said as I got out. I gave her a wave, grabbed my purse, and stepped out onto the curb to face Noah.

"What are you doing here? Are you stalking me now?" I asked, sounding more irritated than I felt.

I was annoyed, but I was more confused. I just wanted Noah to go away. If he kept coming around like this, I wasn't going to be able to keep my distance.

"I don't know," Noah admitted. "I definitely don't want to be creepy stalker guy, Ella. But I haven't seen you for two years. Now, you're only a few blocks away, and I couldn't just sit in my hotel room and wait until tomorrow."

"I don't know what you want from me," I said.

"I want you to give me a chance."

"I'm not agreeing to anything," I said, unlocking the door to let us in. "But you can come in for a little while. We'll have a cup of tea. Then you're leaving."

"That sounds great," Noah said, following me inside.

As we rode up the freight elevator, I tried to think of what I should say. What was there *to* say? He wanted to try again. I wasn't sure that was a good idea.

Understatement.

I was very sure that wasn't a good idea. Noah had shattered my heart the first time we'd broken up. I couldn't handle that again. Or maybe I could handle it, but I didn't want to.

I dropped my purse and keys by the door and went straight to the kitchen to make tea. Dinner had helped, but my head throbbed from the schnapps and then the wine. I wasn't drunk, but I wasn't entirely sober, either. I made tea automatically, choosing what I knew was Noah's favorite, oolong, and my own preferred Earl Grey.

I handed Noah the mug of tea, shoving it into his hand roughly enough that hot water splashed on his skin. He hissed in pain but took the mug. I snatched it back and set it on the counter, quickly wetting a rag with cold water and pressing it to his hand.

"Noah, I'm sorry. I'm so sorry. Did I burn you?"

Noah pulled his hand back and examined the pink skin where the tea had splashed his hand. "It wasn't that hot," he lied.

My shoulders slumped. I was a jerk.

"I'm sorry," I said again. "And I'm sorry I punched you yesterday. I shouldn't have hit you, especially while you were in the middle of a meeting with investors. That wasn't okay."

"It was a little awkward, I'll admit. Did it make you feel better? Hitting me?"

"Am I a total asshole if I admit that it did?" I asked, avoiding his eyes.

Noah took the wet rag from my hand and dropped it on the counter before picking up his tea.

"Not an asshole, Ella. Never an asshole. Just human and angry. You have a right to be angry. Looking back, neither of us handled things very well. We were too young."

"We were young," I agreed. Young enough to think that love solved all problems, healed all wounds. I was old enough now to know that love was a gift, a beautiful, essential gift worth any sacrifice, but it wouldn't solve my problems.

In my experience, love only ended up making everything more complicated.

"Are you willing to consider it?" Noah asked, shaking me out of my reverie.

"Consider what? Getting back together?" I asked.

"I miss you, Els," he said. My heart squeezed when he called me 'Els.' I hadn't heard that nickname in forever.

"How would that even work, Noah? You're in California. I'm here."

"You could come to California," he said.

I stared at him, heart sinking. Had I really hoped we could make this work? I must have, just a little, to feel so let down.

"Noah, I can't. I have to finish school."

He stared at me, not saying what we were both thinking. I wasn't *in* school. I was working as a nanny and freelancing on the side. Even when I managed to save up the money to go back, I still had over a year left.

Stating what I thought was obvious, I said, "I can't move across the country, Noah. What would I do?"

"There are graduate programs out there. Carnegie Mellon has a program right in the valley. You could—"

"Noah," I interrupted. "Stop. Please. It's not the same. You know it isn't."

How could he not get it? He knew how hard I'd worked to get into my program at Tech. It was unique, just like Oliver's project was unique. If I transferred to another school, I could get my degree, but it wouldn't be the same.

Noah cradled his mug and took a sip, his shoulders set, eyes hard. I knew that look. Noah wasn't going to give up. The worst thing was, I wasn't sure I wanted him to.

"I'll wait for you. We can do long distance. Would you be willing to come to California when you finish school?"

"Maybe," I hedged.

"Is it California you're not sure about, or me?" Noah asked, meeting my eyes.

"You," I answered honestly. California sounded great. Thousands of miles away from friends and family if Noah flaked on me again? That part wasn't as appealing.

Noah set his half-empty mug on the counter and crossed the kitchen.

"Then let's see what I can do to change your mind."

It had been a while, but Noah still knew me better than anyone.

His hand slid along my chin, fingers curving around the base of my skull to bury themselves in my hair, sending shivers cascading through my body. His thumb grazed my cheek, and he tilted my face up to his.

One glimpse of the molten heat in those bittersweet chocolate eyes and I was lost.

His lips hit mine in a rush, his mouth taking control of the kiss before my brain realized what was happening. This was the downside of drinking too much. I wasn't drunk, but I was just tipsy enough that my limbic brain was in control.

I didn't want to think.

I didn't want to hurt.

I just wanted to feel.

My long-neglected body roared to life under Noah's hands. My fingers dove into his hair, holding him close as I kissed him back with everything I had.

Letting out a low growl of triumph, Noah lifted me, sitting me on the counter and making space for himself between my legs.

I leaned into him, pasting my torso against his, feeling the heat of his skin through his shirt. Dropping my hands, I found the bottom of the fabric and slipped my fingers beneath, laying my palms against his warm, silky skin. I'd always loved the feel of his skin; the softness stretched over lean muscle.

Noah had been working out in California. The ridges of his abs tempted me. Before I could think better of it, I yanked his shirt up, trying to push it over his head.

Noah ripped it off, breaking our kiss for only a second before his mouth found mine again. All that smooth skin and hard muscle. I touched him everywhere—those broad shoulders, his corded arms.

Noah's hands closed over my hips, yanking me into him, the hard bar of his cock pressing into my heat.

Why was I wearing jeans?

Too many clothes were between us.

Hands streaked up my sides, coming together in the center of my back. A flick of his fingers and my bra fell loose. When he drew my shirt over my head, I lifted my arms. A rush of fire hit between my legs at the touch of his chest to my bare breasts.

Skin to skin.

The rasp of his chest hair on my nipples. The chill of the loft and the heat of Noah's body. I nipped at his neck, smelling him. Ocean and fresh grass. A hint of lemon and mint.

Breathing deeply, I let Noah's scent fill me.

This was Noah.

My Noah.

He lifted me, and I wrapped my legs around his waist. "Where's your bedroom?" he growled in my ear.

"Down the hall," I said.

I didn't question it. Didn't wonder if I should be doing this. It was stupid. He'd broken my heart. He might do it again. But for the first time in two years, I felt whole.

I wanted more.

We were moving, and then we were in my room. Noah set me on my feet and efficiently stripped my jeans over my hips and down my legs. I stepped out of them and fell backward on the bed, bringing him with me. He resisted long enough to grab a condom out of the back pocket of his jeans and shove them off before he joined me.

"Ella," he whispered. "Ella. You feel so good. I missed you so much."

I was dizzy, still a little tipsy, my head spinning from Noah. His hand was between my legs, stroking me, one long finger filling me. He groaned at the clasp of my flesh on his.

"Fuck, Ella. You're so wet." A second finger pressed inside, stretching me, making me ready for him. It had been two years, but I remembered Noah's size. No matter how wet I was, after so many months of celibacy, even his fingers were too much.

The ball of his thumb pressed into my clit, and I gasped, my hips jerking up, burying his fingers deep as pleasure splintered. I was so close. So fucking close.

"Noah, please."

"I've got you, baby," Noah said into my mouth as he kissed me and pressed his thumb again, rotating it in a slow circle as he thrust a third finger inside me. The orgasm exploded in my brain, in my body, like a bomb. I rode his hand, kissing him frantically, every part of me waking up, remembering.

I gasped for breath, still riding the wave of orgasm when Noah withdrew his hand. I keened in disappointment for just a second before he was there, his cock pressing into me.

This. This was what I wanted.

He filled me slowly, sending sparks of bliss through my body. Bracing himself on his elbows, he began to move, the motion so slight he was almost still. The invasion of his thick cock and the teasing rock of his hips were enough to kindle the beginnings of a second orgasm. I arched my back, brushing the tips of my nipples into his chest, and wrapped my legs around his hips.

Nothing was as good as this.

Nothing had ever been as good as Noah.

He kept up the same gentle rhythm, teasing me, ushering me deeper and deeper into pleasure, leaving me gasping and moaning and begging for more. When he hooked a hand behind my knee, opening me wide, and thrust harder, I screamed. The second orgasm took me like a tidal wave, building so slowly and then falling all at once, dragging me deep beneath the surface of pleasure and memory.

I'm sure I didn't pass out. Pretty sure. But it got a little hazy after that. Noah got up and then came back. He slipped into bed beside me, pulling me into his arms, and said, "Ella."

I rolled into him, snuggling my head into his chest, the familiar thump of his heart beneath my ear. "I don't want to talk," I murmured, "I just want to stay like this."

He kissed the top of my head, stroked my hair, and said, "Okay, babe. We don't have to talk."

Content for the first time in two years, I drifted to sleep.

Chapter Seven
Noah

I woke up happier than I'd been in years. Ella's body was nestled against mine, her breasts pillowed into my side, the scent of her shampoo in my nose. For the first time since we'd split up, I felt whole.

I'd thought I was determined to get her back. I hadn't known what true determination was until I lay there with the woman I loved in my arms.

There was no way I was going to lose her again. Whatever I had to do, Ella would be mine.

It was early, and I was content to lay there, my arm around her. As long as she was asleep, I could pretend everything was okay. I had a plan. Okay, I was developing a plan. I'd been honest the day before. I could do long distance.

Ella thought I didn't understand how important school was to her, but I did. I wanted her to be happy. Achieving my own dreams wouldn't mean much if they came at the cost of Ella's. I just had to figure out a way we could both get what we wanted.

Not long after I woke up, she stirred, nuzzling her cheek

into my shoulder and yawning. I knew the second she remembered the night before because her body went stiff. She cleared her throat, drew in a long breath, and relaxed.

Tracing an idle circle over my abs, she asked, "Noah?"

"Yeah?"

"Just making sure I'm actually awake."

"Did you think you were dreaming?"

"For a second," she admitted.

"Good dream? Or nightmare?" I asked, only half-joking. She didn't answer right away.

"I don't know yet. Are you going to disappear on me?"

The hesitant vulnerability in her voice killed me.

"No. Never again. I promise, Ella. We're going to figure this thing out."

"Okay." She pulled away and sat up, sadly taking the sheet with her, covering those perfect breasts. She squinted her eyes at the light coming in from the window and pressed a palm to her forehead.

"You okay?"

"Yeah, I just drank too much last night. Some water and ibuprofen and I'll be fine."

Alarm streaked through me, and I racked my brain for memories of the night before. Had she been drunk? She hadn't seemed drunk. She hadn't even seemed tipsy. She hadn't tasted like she'd been drinking, but she'd had that tea before I kissed her. Had I been so focused on getting her into bed that I hadn't noticed that she wasn't sober enough to decide to sleep with me?

"How much did you have to drink last night?" I asked cautiously.

"Not that much," she said. "I just, you know, I don't drink a lot, so I was a little tipsy, and I forgot to have water before bed."

"How tipsy were you?"

Catching on, Ella gave a gentle shake to her head and said, "Not that tipsy, Noah. I knew what I was doing."

"And you wanted to do it?" I asked.

"Yeah. I definitely did." Ella sank back into the mattress and rolled into me, using my shoulder as a pillow.

I was grateful there was another condom stashed in my jeans. I rolled Ella to her back and rose over her, my eyes greedily absorbing the sight of her naked body. Happily ensconced in my own personal version of heaven, I lowered my mouth to take one rosy nipple inside, sucking and worrying it with my teeth until she squirmed beneath me. Lifting my head, I said, "You know what's really good for a headache?"

Ella laughed. I caught her other nipple between two fingers and squeezed, knowing it would make her squirm again. A few minutes of that, and I wasn't surprised to find her pussy hot and slick and ready. I wanted to fuck her again. I was going to fuck her again. But there was something else I had to do first.

Working my way down the mattress, I spread her thighs wide and hooked her legs over my shoulders.

"Noah," she breathed.

I wasn't going to ask, but she'd been so tight the night before, I doubted there'd been anyone since we split up. I wished I could say the same. I wish I'd never let her get away.

I couldn't go back. We could only go forward. But if she hadn't had sex with anyone in two years, she probably hadn't had this either. Ella liked my mouth between her legs almost as much as I liked having it there. I spread her pussy open with my thumbs, the familiar salty, sweet smell of her going straight to my head, leaving me giddy.

Unable to resist diving right in, my tongue flicked out, tasting her clit. She gasped, and my cock surged beneath me. I gave her clit another long, slow lick, loving the way she squirmed. Her hips started to rock into me, and I gave her what she wanted, licking and sucking, finally fucking her with one finger, then two.

Ella never could stay still when I was eating her pussy. She came hard, gasping my name as she rode my fingers and my tongue. The tight, rhythmic pulses of her body around my fingers were enough to bring me to the edge. I could've come right then, spilling into the sheets like a teenager, but I wanted to fuck her again. I had to.

I was sliding off the bed to get the condom from my jeans when my phone rang. Shit. The ringtone belonged to my chief engineer. I couldn't ignore it. But I was going to.

"Noah?"

"Ignore it. I'll call him back later."

Propped up on one elbow, too sated to realize she was lying there naked, Ella stared at me with sleepy eyes and reached out a hand. I twined my fingers with hers and rose over her, settling between her legs. I was just about to tear open the condom when my phone rang again.

Ella's eyebrows knit together. "Noah, you should get that."

Fuck. Fucking fuck fuck.

I did not want to answer the goddamn phone. I was a breath away from being balls deep in Ella. I did not fucking care about work. The ringtone started up again.

Dave would never call me three times in a row unless something was seriously wrong.

Dropping the open condom on the sheet beside Ella, I rolled over and grabbed my phone out of my jeans. "Dave, what's up, man?"

"Have you seen your email? Twitter? Anything?"

"No," I said, dread building in my chest. Dave was not an emotional guy, yet he sounded frantic. "What's going on? Everything was fine when I went to bed last night."

"Yeah, well, sometime in the middle of the night, your old friend Philip Martin got another bug up his ass. Let me read you the first tweet and save you some time. *Just learned Endicott Tech has a new product based off their stolen code. #Criminalsgofree.* And then right after that *Also heard Endicott's looking for investors. Hope they like lawsuits. #Highrisknoreward.*"

"Are you fucking kidding me?"

Out of the corner of my eye, I saw Ella get out of bed and disappear into the bathroom. How could things be so perfect one second and so utterly fucked up the next? I'd long since given up trying to figure out what Philip Martin's problem was.

My best guess went back to adolescent resentment combined with the crush he had on Ella in college. I'd never stolen a goddamn thing from anyone. Particularly not from Philip Martin, who didn't have the skills to create a program like the one I'd used to found Endicott Tech. The lawsuit had been mostly bullshit from the start.

He'd cribbed together notes from some projects we worked on in undergrad and some emails that looked incriminating taken out of context but had nothing to do with anything in reality. I hadn't settled because I was guilty. I'd settled because the lawsuit was fucking expensive and there were better things I could do with Endicott Tech's money than spend it on lawyers.

I did not need this now.

Taking a deep breath, I said to Dave, "Is there anything else, other than the tweets?"

"Not yet, but they're being retweeted like crazy."

"Anyone sticking up for us?" I asked.

"Some," Dave said." Everyone who knows us, knows Martin, is defending us, but you know the Internet. That still leaves a lot of assholes with no fucking clue and a big platform to jump on Martin's bandwagon. I'm afraid to ask how the meeting with Winters went."

"I'm optimistic," I said. "Though this isn't going to help. Winters hates the media. If he invests with us and this kind of shit keeps going on, he runs the risk of getting dragged into it."

"Can we shut Martin down?" Dave asked.

"No. We can't afford to buy him off. And we can't afford to sue him. We need every penny to keep the company going until we crack the code."

"I may have good news on that front, at least," Dave said.

"Really? I could use some good news. Lay it on me."

"We think we may have figured out a way around that bug that was disabling phones too close to the transmitter. We haven't done full testing yet, but the few times we tried it before we all passed out last night, it worked."

Dave's voice vibrated with triumph and anticipation. This was huge. Our software—and the transmitter we were developing—would give property owners the ability to incapacitate a drone almost instantly, forcing it to land itself and ignore commands, either preprogrammed or delivered from its remote.

That sounded great, and we'd already been selling limited versions of it overseas. More and more, terrorists and wackos were using drones to attack. Imagine a drone, armed with a chemical weapon, programmed to land in the courtyard of a school or a stadium. The potential for devastation was terrifyingly high.

Unfortunately, the technology we used to force the drone to ignore its mission and land also interfered with local Wi-Fi signals, which was a violation of federal law. If we couldn't get the technology to work in compliance with United States law, we couldn't sell it here. We had a long list of buyers ready and waiting, from the federal government to NFL owners and schools of all levels.

We were so close to working out the last of the bugs. If Dave thought they'd isolated the Wi-Fi interference issue, we might be able to move into the final stages of testing. It wouldn't be fast enough to do without additional funds, but hell, after Dave's other news, any progress on the project was great.

"Call me as soon as you give it another roll and feel like you have a handle on where we are. I'll keep my phone with me."

"And the tweets? Do we respond?"

"No. For now, let's just ignore him. We know our code is 100% original. So does he. If the rest of the Internet wants to work themselves into a frenzy over it, let them. If Vance holds this against us, I'll have to figure something else out. But we need to keep our eyes on the ball. We're too close to let Martin distract us."

"Got it, boss. I'll keep you posted." Dave hung up.

I sat on the edge of the bed, staring at the hardwood floor between my feet. At the sound of the bathroom door opening, I looked up to meet Ella's eyes.

"What's going on?" She pulled on a worn flannel robe that was sexy as hell when wrapped around her body. I wanted to strip it off and drag her back to bed, but I had a feeling the mood was broken. "You want me to make coffee?" she asked.

"That would be great."

I jumped in the shower and got dressed in the clothes I'd worn the day before. I didn't want to leave. I didn't want to end this interlude with Ella, but it looked like my day would be all about damage control thanks to Philip fucking Martin. Ella, bless her, had a hot cup of coffee waiting for me.

"Is everything okay?" she asked. I didn't want to dump this crap on her, but it wasn't fair to try to protect her either. She should know what was going on.

"You remember Philip Martin? He tweeted out a bunch of bullshit last night, trying to get people stirred up against Endicott."

Guilt flooded her eyes, and I tensed. In an anguished voice, she said, "Noah, I'm so sorry. I meant to tell you and then . . . we got distracted. He called me last night. Philip did. When Tate and Emily were driving me home."

"What? What did he want? What did he say to you?"

"He said he was calling to warn me that you were in town, but I really think he was trying to find out if you'd met with Vance. He knew I worked for them. He said he's had an eye on you because you're bidding for the same jobs."

"What a load of bullshit," I spat out. "We're not bidding for the same jobs. He works in social media development. Nothing he does is in any way related to Endicott Tech. Has he called you before?"

"Not recently," she said. "He called me once right after he sued you, but I hung up on him. It was really weird, Noah. He was acting like we were good friends, telling me he was worried about me, worried that you were going to bother me while you were here, but then he knew where I worked and started asking me questions about you and Vance. Creepy."

"I don't like this," I said. "You know he had a crush on

you in college, right?"

"Philip Martin? What? I didn't even know him that well."

"We got in a fight about you once when I overheard him making comments I didn't appreciate. And after we broke up, he used to throw you in my face all the time whenever we ran into each other—which was too often because of that stupid fucking lawsuit. He must've heard a rumor that we were close to hitting the market with our new software. But how the hell did he know I was here?"

"Could someone on your team be talking? Even if it's not on purpose. You know how everyone knows each other. Maybe someone said something to a friend and the friend works with Martin. He said he's had eyes on you," Ella said.

"That could mean anything," I said. "He makes good money. He could've hired someone to watch me. I know that sounds crazy, but this is Philip Martin we're talking about. He tried to sink my company just because he thought he could. I wouldn't put it past him to do something crazy, but he's got shit timing, as always."

"Is there anything I can do to help?" Ella asked, her gaze open and sincere. I wanted to say, *Yeah, you can ask your boss to give me the money I need, or at least put in a good word for me.*

I didn't do it. I didn't want Ella mixed up in my business, especially not with Philip Martin calling her. If Martin was involved, I didn't want Ella anywhere near this mess.

"Yes," I said. "You can say you'll have dinner with me tonight. I was serious when I said I want to figure this out, Ella. I know it's complicated. We're on different sides of the country. You have to finish school. My company sucks up a lot of time, and I know that's not ideal. If we don't get this product to market soon, we're going to be scrambling. And if we do get it to market, we're going to be busting our asses to keep up with demand. Either way, the next year or so is going to be stressful and crazy. That's part of why I kept putting off coming back here. I want to be able to tell you that I can put you first. And in my heart, Ella, you'll always be first. But there are going to be times when the company gets in the way. I didn't handle that very well before. I know I can do better now."

"I'll have dinner with you," she said quietly. "I'll have dinner with you, and we can talk."

"I'll pick you up here at seven?" I asked, feeling like I'd won the lottery despite the cluster fuck that had hit this morning.

"Seven," Ella agreed.

My phone beeped an alert. A text from Vance Winters. Shit.

Caught Twitter this morning. This doesn't look good, Noah. Call me.

Even Vance's ominous text couldn't dull my mood.

Putting him out of my mind temporarily, I said, "Do you need to get your car? I have to get moving, but if you get dressed, I'll drop you off."

Ella's smile, sweet and hopeful, was enough to set me up for the rest of the day.

I dropped her off at her car with the promise to see her later and headed back to the Four Seasons to change clothes and get to work. Between Endicott Tech, fucking Philip Martin, a call with Vance Winters, and the plans I had for Ella, I had a lot to do, and not a lot of time.

I knew how to crush a deadline.

Flipping open my laptop, I ordered up breakfast and got to work.

CHAPTER EIGHT
ELLA

T floated through my day, trying to pretend to myself that I wasn't daydreaming about Noah. The night before had been . . . I have no words.

Familiar and yet new.

Back when Noah and I first started having sex, we'd been kids. Over the legal age, but not adults. Not really. What we'd lacked in knowledge, we'd made up for in enthusiasm.

I'd never been disappointed in Noah—not when we were in bed. Still, as good as it had been back then, now, sex with Noah was a whole different ballgame. I felt bad that the phone call had interrupted us that morning. I'd been treated to a spectacular orgasm thanks to Noah's very talented mouth, and he'd been left with nothing.

I had plans to make it up to him.

He hadn't told me anything about where we were going, so I had no idea what to wear. I'd texted him that afternoon to ask, and his answer had been less than helpful.

There is no dress code. Wear whatever you want.

Noah was great in bed, but sometimes, I thought he

didn't know much about women. I settled for a shift dress with spaghetti straps and a V-neckline. It wasn't short, exactly, but it hit a few inches above the knee with a swirly skirt that showed more leg when I moved my hips.

The dress itself wasn't a showstopper, though I thought I looked good in it. No, the real reason I chose it was what I was wearing beneath. I hadn't had much cause to wear lingerie in the past few years. What I was wearing I'd actually purchased a few months before Noah and I had split up, but because he hadn't had time to come home and I'd had a hard time getting out to California, he'd never seen it.

At the memory of our failure at long distance, I felt a twinge of unease.

But we were different people now, weren't we?

If we really wanted to, we could handle this. I needed to believe that was true.

I was touching up my lip gloss in the bathroom mirror when the buzzer at the front door rang. Tossing the lip gloss in a small purse, I grabbed my keys and hit the button on the intercom. "I'll be right down."

I opened the door to see Noah standing outside, wearing a navy blue suit and a blue- and green-patterned tie. Except for his college graduation, I'd never seen Noah in a suit. My mouth went dry at the sight of that lean, built body wrapped up in a perfectly tailored suit.

I liked Noah as he usually was, in his faded jeans and Converse high-tops, but I wouldn't complain if he wanted to dress up every once in a while. Not if this was the result.

I locked the door behind me and turned back to see him staring at me.

"What?"

He recovered himself and slid an arm around my waist

to lead me to the car, parked just up the block in the entrance to the alley.

"You look beautiful," he said.

Warmth flushed my cheeks. "Thank you."

I let Noah open my door and help me into the car. As he pulled back out into the street, I asked, "Where are we going?"

"Not far," he said. Still being mysterious.

A few minutes later, we pulled into the lower parking deck of the Four Seasons Hotel. I expected Noah to head for the restaurant, not the elevators.

"Is there someplace to eat up here?" I asked.

Looking a little nervous, Noah swallowed hard and said, "There is."

I got it a few minutes later when Noah led me into his suite. I might have been annoyed at him for making assumptions, but we'd slept together the night before, and it's not like that was the first time. Besides, he'd gone to a lot of effort.

There were flowers everywhere, roses, lilies, and the Gerber daisies I'd always loved best. A bottle of champagne sat chilling in an ice bucket beside two crystal glasses. The desk had been turned into an elegant dining table, complete with a linen tablecloth, fine china, and a chair on either side. Tucked against the wall of the sitting room, I spotted a room service cart stacked with covered dishes.

In explanation, Noah said, "I wanted to be alone with you. I didn't want to share you with an entire restaurant, and room service here is very accommodating. But if you'd rather go out—"

"No, this is beautiful. Thank you."

"Are you hungry?" Noah asked.

Was I? I wasn't sure I could tell. My senses were so

focused on his nearness, the scent of the flowers, and the effort he'd put into making dinner special. I shrugged one shoulder.

"If you're hungry, I could eat."

"Okay. First, I wanted to give you this."

Noah disappeared into the bedroom of the suite and returned a moment later with an unsealed envelope in his hand. His shoulders were tense, his eyes flicking from the envelope to me and back again.

He was nervous. My stomach tightened in anticipation of bad news.

I opened the envelope and drew out two pieces of paper, the contents familiar but entirely unexpected. It was a course schedule for spring semester. The exact classes I'd been enrolled in before I'd been forced to drop out. I turned the class schedule over in my hands, trying to understand, and saw the sheet of paper beneath. A statement from the bursar's office showing the semester's tuition had been paid, including living expenses and a dining card.

I stared at the papers, my chest tight. Looking up at Noah, I asked, "What is this? What did you do?"

Noah shoved his hands in his pockets. "I enrolled you in school and paid your tuition."

"But . . . you can't do that. Why would you do that?"

"Because I love you, Ella. Because I can. I'm sure that you're an amazing nanny for Vance and Maggie. But that's not what you should be doing with your life. You belong back in school."

"I know that. I know, and I've been working on it. You didn't have to—"

"I know I didn't have to," Noah exploded, yanking his hands out of his pockets and throwing them out to his sides. "And I know you probably don't want my money. I don't care. This isn't a loan. This is a gift. For you. Because I love you and I want you to be happy."

"Noah," I said, and trailed off. I didn't know how to take it in. Ever since I'd dropped out, ever since I'd realized how hard it was to pay off the loans, getting back to school had felt like a pipe dream. No matter how determined I was, with every day that passed, it seemed further out of reach.

And now, Noah had handed me back my dreams.

"Look, there are no strings, okay? If you want to walk out that door, if you decide this isn't going to work and you never want to see me again, I still have your tuition paid until you graduate. You can throw it in my face and walk away if you want to. As long as you show up for school in January."

I stared down at those two pieces of paper covered in simple black and white print that changed the course of my life. Sometime between that morning and now, while Noah had been handling his own crisis with his company, he'd found the time to give me the one thing I wanted more than anything else.

More than anything . . . except for him.

Carefully, I folded the pages back up and slid them into the envelope. I folded the envelope in thirds and slipped it into my purse, zipping it closed. I knew later, when I was alone, I'd pull them out and stare at them to reassure myself that they were real.

"I don't know what to say. Thank you doesn't seem like enough."

"I thought you'd be mad."

"I'm confused. Not mad. That was a lot of money, Noah. The whole reason you're here is to try to get funding for your company, and then you go and spend all that money on me."

"The money doesn't mean anything, Ella, if I can't use it to give the woman I love her dreams back. Either things will work out with Vance, or they won't. There are other investors. There's only one you."

I stared at Noah, taking in the sincerity in his eyes and the relief that I wasn't angry. We had a lot to work out between us, but right then, I knew what I wanted. I wanted to say thank you.

"Is dinner going to get cold?" I asked, eyeing the room service cart.

Noah shook his head.

I reached behind me and lowered the zipper on my dress, dipping my right shoulder until the narrow strap fell to my arm and the bodice sagged. As the zipper reached my hips, I dipped my left shoulder and the top of the dress slipped to my waist, revealing a black satin bustier trimmed in matching lace.

With a deliberate shimmy of my hips, I shook off the dress, stepping away from my discarded clothes. I stood there for a moment, loving the way Noah's pupils dilated and his breath grew shallow as he took in the sight of me wearing the black lingerie and spike heels.

I took a step toward him, reaching for the lapels of his suit coat. Before he had a chance to react, I pulled it down over his shoulders. He shook it off, leaving me free to go to work on his tie.

His dark eyes dazed, he said, "Ella, you don't have to . . . I didn't bring you here just so we could—"

"I know I don't have to, Noah. I want to. You had to leave this morning before we could finish. You took care of me, and I never got to take care of you."

He swallowed hard and went to work on the buttons of his shirt. It didn't take long, between the two of us, before he was naked. I looked around the room and got an idea. Noah reached for me, but I swatted his hand away and said, "Here. Come here."

I led him to the open space beside the couch, diagonally across from a full-length mirror. Pressing my hands up to his shoulders, I pushed him back, so he was half leaning against the wall.

Before he could protest, I dropped to my knees. Looking to the side, I saw us reflected in the mirror, head to toe. I knew Noah got it when he looked down at me and then over at the mirror, swearing under his breath.

I had to admit, we made a striking picture, me with my hair up, my lips glossy pink, my breasts spilling out over the black satin bustier, on my knees in front of Noah, his hard cock inches from my mouth.

I licked my lips, watching in the mirror as his chest hitched with a strangled breath and his eyelids lowered over his dark eyes.

Noah towered above me, his posture dominating but oddly still. He had me on my knees, but I was in control. And what a man to have before me, with his tall body, strong legs, defined chest, and the six-pack he'd somehow managed to acquire out in California.

I'd loved him when he was a gangly teenager. Seeing him like this made me dizzy with lust.

Turning my eyes away from the mirror, I put all of my attention where I wanted it. On the thick, very hard cock in front of my mouth. I'd heard girls say they didn't like performing oral sex. Maybe if it were another guy, I wouldn't either. But I'd always loved putting my mouth on Noah.

I started with a kiss. The head of his cock was dark red, a bead of pre-come already rising up to meet my tongue. His balls were drawn tight to his body. He wanted this as much as I did.

I didn't have it in me to tease. Not this time. This time, I just wanted to feel Noah come.

I was way out of practice, but I did my best, taking him in my mouth as far as I could and sucking hard, loving the taste of him, the earthy maleness all wrapped up in Noah's sea salt and fresh grass scent.

He was mine. This cock was mine. I cupped his balls in one hand and wrapped the other tightly around the base of his cock, smoothing the moisture from my mouth up and down his length, so my hand slid easily as I sucked him.

Above me, Noah groaned my name and sank his fingers into my hair, sending pins flying. The long strands tumbled down my back. He held them out of my face, staring down at me with hungry, hot eyes.

I glanced to the side to catch sight of us in the mirror, and my pussy flooded with heat. He wasn't looking at the mirror. —he was looking down at me, his breathing ragged, his hips starting to jerk, thrusting his cock against the back of my throat.

I'd never been able to take him all the way, and I couldn't do it now, so out of practice. Noah tightened his grip on my head and tried to pull me back. I sucked harder, refusing to be budged.

I wanted him out of control.

I wanted him overwhelmed.

I needed him to lose himself in me.

His cock pulsed in my mouth, spilling salty heat over my tongue. I swallowed hard, again and again, working his length with my mouth until he was done.

His breath was still short when I lay a last kiss on his

cock and wobbled to my feet. I hadn't come, but I was seriously turned on.

I'd had more orgasms in the last twenty-four hours than I'd had in the previous twenty-four months, and I wanted more. I was greedy for Noah. I had been since that first kiss in Vance and Maggie's kitchen. I was beginning to understand that I would always be greedy for Noah. His heart, his mind, and his body.

"Dinner?" I asked.

In a low voice, Noah said, "Only if you're wearing that."

"I'm definitely wearing this," I said.

I expected Noah to grab a robe or put on his boxers, but he did neither. Totally comfortable with being stark naked, he opened the champagne, poured two glasses, and sat me at the table, holding out my chair as if we were in a fine restaurant.

Dinner was sushi, and even after our distraction, it was at the perfect serving temperature. Just like he still knew my favorite coffee house drink was chai tea, Noah hadn't forgotten a single one of my favorite sushi rolls. He'd even managed to get Toro sashimi, the strips of fatty tuna an indulgent luxury we'd rarely been able to afford when we were college students.

The meal was a flashback, so much like all the other meals we'd shared before that I had the odd sense of being in a time warp. We ate off each other's plates and told each other about our days, laughing at stupid things no one else would find funny.

Noah was cagey when I brought up Philip Martin, insisting that he had the situation under control. When I asked him what he'd done, he admitted, "I'm not doing anything. If I protest or try to set the record straight, it just gives Philip more ammunition. I need to stay focused and not let him distract me."

"But will he stop?" I asked. "What will you do if all of this changes Vance and Maggie's minds about investing in Endicott Tech?"

Noah shrugged and looked away. "It would be inconvenient, but not the end of the world. We'll figure it out. I don't want to talk about work tonight."

"Do you want to talk about us?" I asked, my heart pounding in my chest. I wasn't sure I was ready to talk about us, but if I didn't face reality, I was no better than the girl who let Noah slip through her fingers two years before.

"That depends on how the talk goes," he said, a hesitantly flirty glint in his eyes.

"I want to know how you see this working," I said. "It's going to be over a year before I can leave Atlanta for good. Your life is in California."

"It's not going to be easy," Noah admitted. "I already hate the idea of leaving you. But I can't abandon my people. We have too much on the line."

"Noah, I don't expect you to walk away from everything you've built out there. I guess I just want some kind of guarantee that you're not going to run out of here and forget about me."

"Ella, I could never forget about you. That's not what happened back then. I just did a shitty job of balancing work and you. I know better now. Whatever happens with the business, I can afford to travel back and forth. I'll make the time. When you're on school break, I'll fly you out. If you think you want to relocate, you'll want to spend time out there anyway, get to know people, see if you like the house or if you want to move. We can start building a life together if that's what you want."

"It *is* what I want," I said, my heart in my throat.

Saying those words was a head-first dive off the side of a skyscraper, desperately hoping Noah would swoop through the air and save me before the concrete below smashed me to bits.

The last time we'd been here, he'd said all the right words, just like he was now. Then he'd gotten on a plane and gradually forgotten about me.

I wanted to believe that wouldn't happen this time.

I wanted to believe things would be different.

My heart trusted Noah, but my head was already having second thoughts.

I shoved those second thoughts aside for the rest of the night. Only time would tell, and doubting Noah now wasn't going to help.

He fed me half of the chocolate cake that was my favorite dessert before leading me to bed where he finally unhooked the bustier, stripped off the satin thong, and made love to me, thoroughly, twice. Like I had the night before, I fell asleep in his arms, lulled by the familiar comfort of his heartbeat.

And exactly like the morning before, the ring of his phone interrupted just as we were getting to the good stuff.

I had his cock in my hand, his fingers between my legs, and his mouth on my breast when his phone went crazy. Beeping, then ringing, then beeping again. He ignored it until the room phone joined in. Rolling away, growling "Fuck," under his breath, Noah snagged the phone off the bedside table and said, "What?"

Whatever he heard on the other end must have been bad, because his face drained of color and he sat up in a rush of movement that yanked the sheets from my body and sent his pillows flying to the floor. His spine was as stiff as his voice as he said, "Uh-huh. Uh-huh. Yeah, okay. Do what you can to contain the situation. I'll call you back later."

"Noah, what's going on? Is everything okay?" I asked stupidly since it was clear something was very much not okay.

Noah stood, not meeting my eyes, and strode for the bathroom. "I'm good. I need to take a shower. Everything's fine, but I'm going to have to get to work."

I pulled the sheet back to cover me. "What happened? Who was that?"

Noah stopped outside the bathroom door, his face blank, eyes shuttered. "It was Dave, the lead on the drone project."

"What's wrong?"

"Nothing, Ella. Just a bug in the software." He drummed his fingers against the door frame, impatient to get moving.

"He wouldn't have called that many times over a bug. Why are you lying to me?"

Noah flinched, fear flashing from his eyes before he got himself under control and said, "I'm not lying, Ella. Everything's fine. I just need to get to work, okay?"

I watched him disappear into the bathroom with narrowed eyes. He *was* lying. He knew it, and I knew it.

Noah had always been a shitty liar, not that he'd made a habit of being dishonest. He was one of the most moral men I knew, which was probably why he was so bad at hiding the truth.

Sitting in the middle of the big bed, holding the sheet to my chest, I felt dismissed. Unnecessary. In the way.

Whatever was wrong, it was obvious that Noah didn't want to talk about it. I didn't expect him to tell me everything. He had a right to keep things to himself. I knew that.

That didn't help the sense that things were sliding out of my control once again.

This was how it had started before. Everything was good, and then Noah was too busy for me. Too busy to talk. Too busy to let me in.

Slowly, I got out of the bed and started pulling on my clothes. I had to have a little faith in him. I couldn't doubt him every time things didn't go perfectly or we wouldn't make it a month.

By the time he got out of the shower, I was dressed, my purse in hand, ready to go.

Noah barely looked at me. "Sorry about this," he said in a rush. "I'll run you home."

"I can get an Uber," I offered, hoping he didn't take me up on it. It wouldn't take him long to drive me home, and calling for an Uber in last night's cocktail dress felt too much like the walk of shame.

I was already feeling pushed aside. I wasn't up to *that*.

"No, I've got you," Noah said.

He drove a little too fast on the way back to Vance's loft, clearly eager to drop me off and start dealing with whatever crisis had popped up, a crisis he was determined not to share.

His kiss goodbye was perfunctory and distracted. I tried not to take it as a sign of things to come, but it was hard.

My heart ached, and my head butted in, always eager to say, *I told you so.*

CHAPTER NINE

ELLA

Dealing with a not quite one-year-old baby is a great way to get your mind off your troubles. Rosie was adorable, with sleek black hair and a rosebud mouth. She was also sweet and cuddly, and an evil little demon when she wanted to be.

As I tried to coax her into opening her mouth for a spoonful of mashed peas, I reflected that nothing turned my angelic little charge into a devil faster than vegetables. She was eyeing the jar of peaches at my elbow, her chubby little arm reaching out. I knew what she was saying.

I don't want these peas, but if you open those peaches, I'll eat every bite, promise.

Scout, Maggie's little boxer/corgi mix, paced back and forth beneath Rosie's high-chair, hoping Rosie would toss him a snack. He'd prefer a cracker, but he'd take a piece of banana. Rosie adored Scout and would happily feed him from her tray the second my back was turned. When she moved up to real food, Scout was going to gain fifty pounds.

Rosie babbled, "Lala. Lala," pointing at the peaches

with a plaintive expression. I love the way she said my name, Lala, but I wasn't budging on the peas.

Most meals, Rosie switched between soft baby food and chomping on solids. I wasn't surprised when she turned her attention to the sliced banana I'd set out in case she wasn't in the mood for peaches. She'd eat fruit for me all day, but the second I showed her anything green, those rosebud lips slammed shut.

I made another approach with the spoon, making choo-choo noises as I aimed for her mouth. A chubby arm came up, batting the spoon out of the way. Used to Rosie's antics, I evaded her, saving myself from a face full of mashed peas.

"Is she giving you trouble?" Maggie asked as she walked in, shrugging out of her jacket and setting her purse on the kitchen island.

"Who, Rosie?" I asked, winking at Maggie. "Never. You know how much she loves her veggies."

Maggie made a sound in the back of her throat that was somewhere between a snort and a laugh. "Check this out," she said, pulling her phone from her purse and flicking through images on the screen. She turned it to show me Vance, scowling, his blonde hair pulled back, his handsome face speckled with orange.

"When did that happen?" I asked. Vance knew his daughter well, and he was usually fast enough to avoid her tricks. Maggie laughed, smiling affectionately at the image of her husband bathed in mashed vegetables.

"Last night. She was hungry, and he decided he should encourage her to eat carrots. I don't know why. He hates carrots. I did get her to eat some green beans, but he got it in his mind that she just needed to try the carrots again."

"I guess she showed him," I said.

Rosie reached out a chubby fist toward the bananas and said, "Na-na! Na-na!"

"Little dictator," I said with a laugh as I got an idea. I picked up a circle of sliced banana, dipped it in the peas, and held it out. Rosie gave me a suspicious look but obediently opened her mouth. She accepted the banana and began to chew.

"Will you look at that?" Maggie said in wonder.

We both smiled at Rosie, smug smiles of adult satisfaction at bending a child to our will. Our smiles faded as Rosie began to scowl. She swallowed the banana/pea combination I'd coaxed her to eat, but when I offered her another, she pressed her lips together and glared at me.

Maggie shrugged. "It was a good idea," she said.

"Is everything set for Vance's show?" I asked. "Did you get lunch?"

Maggie sighed and rolled her eyes. "If she didn't do such a good job, it would be impossible to tolerate that woman."

I knew exactly who she was talking about. Sloan Stevens managed all of Vance's shows, and while she was excellent at selling art, she was a raging bitch, and she hated Maggie.

Sloan had put the moves on Vance more than once, and she'd never forgiven Maggie for not only stealing his heart but taking his name.

Vance's voice cut in, coming from the office down the hall. I couldn't make out each individual word, but he sounded pissed off. Maggie shot a concerned glance in his direction. "I'm going to make us some lunch," she said. "Do you want anything?"

I shook my head. I hadn't been hungry all day. The way Noah and I parted had left me with a sick feeling in my stomach that I couldn't shake.

It got worse when we clearly heard Vance say, "This does not look good, Endicott. You realize that, right? We're in the middle of a negotiation. This is not the time to leave town."

Vance's voice had gradually increased in volume, and I realized why when he stepped into the doorway of the kitchen. His angry blue eyes softened when they saw Maggie, then narrowed in concern when they landed on me.

He saw Maggie organizing sandwich ingredients, winked at her, and disappeared back down the hall, but not before leaning down to drop a kiss on his daughter's head. The kiss brought his phone in earshot, and I heard Noah's voice on the other end, talking fast, stress bleeding from every word.

I scooped another spoonful of peas and tried to distract Rosie into eating them. My heart heavy, tears pricking my eyelids, I wasn't fast enough to evade her when she smacked the spoon. Wet clumps of peas splashed onto my face.

A tear leaked out of the corner of my eye. He was leaving? He'd just promised he wasn't going to run out, and he was leaving? Had he known he was leaving this morning? Was that why he wouldn't tell me what the phone call had been about?

I'd told him I'd trust him. I wanted to trust him.

He wasn't making it easy.

I squeezed my eyes shut tight, fighting back tears. When I opened them, Maggie was in front of me, holding a wet kitchen towel.

I reached for it, but she pulled it back, saying, "Hold on, she got your ponytail."

Gently, Maggie cleaned the peas from my hair.

Obedient as a child, I closed my eyes and tilted my face up as she swiped the cloth over my cheeks and forehead.

"Are you and Noah trying to work things out?" she asked quietly.

"I thought we were," I admitted.

"He didn't say anything about having to leave?" she asked.

"No, but I was with him last night, and the phone was ringing like crazy this morning, and then he wouldn't tell me what it was about."

I didn't want to say too much, though, in truth, I didn't know anything. But, as much as I loved Vance and Maggie, I wouldn't be able to forgive myself if something I said messed up Noah's chances with them.

Maggie folded the pea-encrusted towel and set it down on the table beside Rosie's lunch. "Why don't you go talk to him? I'll finish feeding Rosie. This afternoon is flexible until around two-thirty when I have an appointment, and Vance has to go to the gallery."

"You don't mind? I'll be back by two, probably before."

"No, Ella, it's no big deal. Better to talk to him and find out what's going on. Otherwise, you'll drive yourself crazy worrying and waiting for him to tell you."

I stood, brushing off my jeans and sweater. "Am I good?" I asked.

Maggie gave me a quick head to toe scan, searching for errant globs of baby food. I'd learned—we'd all learned—that feeding Rosie was a contact sport. It was almost impossible to escape without the evidence somewhere on our clothes or in our hair. Usually, in the last place I'd think to look until I was out in public and someone politely commented that I had mashed pears smeared on my shoulder.

"All clear," Maggie promised. "Good luck."

I had the sinking feeling that I would need it.

I tried to call Noah on the way to his hotel but didn't get an answer. When my phone rang in my hand, my heart jumped, sure it was him. Instead, I saw the same number I'd answered two nights before.

Philip Martin.

Why wouldn't he just go away? Irritated and exasperated, I answered and said "Hello?"

"Ella, it's Philip."

"Philip, is something wrong? Why are you calling?"

"I wanted to make sure everything was all right, Ella. And let you know that you won't have to worry about Noah for much longer. He'll be leaving Atlanta shortly, and there won't be any reason for him to go back."

"Philip, what did you do?"

"Nothing that you need to worry about, Ella. I just wanted to make sure you knew that you could relax. Noah isn't going to bother you anymore."

"Philip, I don't need your help with Noah. He's not bothering me."

"You've always been too nice where Noah was concerned," Philip said, a bite in his voice. Something in his tone reminded me of the way he was in college. I didn't know him well, but he was a friend of friends, and we ran into each other here and there.

Philip was always one of those people who lacked the capacity to pick up on social cues. I'd been surprised when he'd gone to work for a social media company since I always thought of them as being about communication.

Communication was not Philip's strong suit.

Neither was reading between the lines. It was against my nature to be rude, but I was tired of Philip thinking that somehow, we were on the same side.

"Philip, Noah isn't bothering me. Actually, we're back together, not that it's any of your business. Why are you going after him like this? First, the lawsuit—which we both know was completely unfounded—and then all those tweets the other night? Why would you do this? Why do you have it in for Noah?"

Heavy silence hung in the air before Philip shot back, "How can you even ask me that, Ella? Don't you remember what it was like in school? Every grant I applied for, Noah got. Every time we shared a project, he was voted lead. He had you before I even had a chance to ask you out. He always got everything I wanted. Now I'm stopping him from getting what he wants."

"Do you even hear yourself?" I asked, incredulous. "This stuff is ancient history, Philip. You've been out of college for three years. You have a great job. And you're not just going after Noah. He has employees, people who need their jobs. You're punishing all of them over some stupid grudge you should've let go of years ago."

"Ella, I always thought you were so smart. Why are women so fucking dumb when it comes to Noah Endicott? I don't get it. You're willing to forgive him anything. Don't you remember what he was like after you two broke up? He fucked his way through California. He dumped you the second he got out here, and he never looked back. Now he's in Atlanta for three days, and you're falling all over yourself to get back together with him? I wasted my time calling you."

"I think you did," I agreed. "You need to stop this, Philip. Leave Noah alone."

"Not going to happen. Have a nice life, Ella."

Philip disconnected the call. I dropped my phone in the center console of my car, staring blindly at the road ahead while I tried to make sense of my conversation with Philip.

I'd never thought of Philip Martin as a nice guy. He was too prickly and insensitive to fall into that category, but I never realized he was a raging lunatic. He hadn't even argued when I'd reminded him that his lawsuit against Noah had been groundless.

There was no point. He knew it, I knew it, and Noah knew it. Everyone knew it. He'd only had enough evidence to blacken Noah's name and drag it out long enough to get some money out of Endicott Technologies.

I racked my brain, trying to remember if I'd ever done anything to encourage Philip's interest. Noah had mentioned a time or two that he thought Philip had a crush on me, but I'd always blown him off. Philip never singled me out or behaved inappropriately, and I'd been too wrapped up in Noah and school to care.

I pulled into the parking lot of the hotel, my thoughts snagging on something Philip had said.

He'll be leaving Atlanta shortly, and there won't be any reason for him to go back.

What had Philip done? Was he the reason Noah was leaving town in a rush? I wouldn't have any answers until I spoke to Noah.

If Philip was set on going after Noah and Endicott Tech, Noah was going to need all of his attention to deal with it, especially with the company in such a vulnerable place.

I wanted Noah. I wanted this to work. But maybe, with everything going on, Noah would be better off if I just let him go.

I heard Noah's voice on the other side of his hotel room door as I raised my hand to knock. It got louder, then he swung the door open, and his eyes widened. He stepped back to invite me in, giving me a look of confusion before he turned his attention back to his call.

"Yeah, yeah. I'll be there. I don't know what he thinks he's going to prove with this, but we'll figure it out, Dave. We're not going to let that fucking weasel drag us down. Yeah, no, I know. I'll text you when I have a time. Okay. Yeah, okay."

He hung up and shoved his phone in his back pocket. It immediately started ringing again. With a look of annoyance, he took it out, checked the screen, and silenced the call.

"Ella, what's going on? Why are you here? I thought you had to work today."

His eyes jumped from mine to the couch opposite the desk. His suitcase sat there, half-open, neat stacks of clothing inside.

Stating the obvious, I said, "You're leaving?"

Noah ran a hand through his hair, looking exasperated and frustrated.

"Els, I have to. I know the timing sucks. I do. But I have to get back to California. Phillips is out there stirring up shit, trying to kill this deal with Winters. It's complete bullshit, but my team heard a rumor that he's planning a protest tomorrow. I can't leave them to deal with that on their own. It's my company. I can't look like I'm hiding."

"A protest? What the hell is there to protest about?" I asked, thoroughly confused. "Are you guys using child labor for your programmers? Doing animal testing?"

A ghost of a smile flitted across Noah's face before he let out a sigh. "No, that's what's so annoying about it. Philip has people spreading a rumor that the software we're developing doesn't incapacitate drones but it enables the NSA to get into the encrypted content of any mobile device within range. He's stirring people up who think we're stealing their data and handing it over to the NSA."

I shook my head. That didn't make any sense. "But isn't that the opposite of what your software does? I thought your software was valuable because it was going to let people disable a drone without touching nearby devices."

"Well, if you're going to be accurate, then yes. Clearly, truth is not a requirement when it comes to getting people to go crazy on social media. Though Dave is pretty sure that Philip is manufacturing most of it by using bot accounts and hired protesters. There are people out there who know what's going on, and they're trying to stick up for us, but they're getting drowned out by Philip's minions. The whole thing is a fucking waste of time, but we can't afford for him to tank Endicott Tech's reputation. Not right now."

"Did he kill the deal with Vance?" I asked cautiously. Noah threw his tall body onto the couch beside his suitcase and shrugged.

"It's hard to say. Officially, no. But he's not impressed. He's not interested in getting dragged into a media feeding frenzy. I don't blame him."

I leaned against the desk and looked at my feet. Everything was a mess. Noah was fighting for his company, for the people who trusted him with their futures.

I wanted to ask him to stay, but I wouldn't. I wouldn't be selfish like that. He was right; he needed to be back home. He needed to show his face if they were going to have any success in overcoming Phillip's smear campaign.

I was just in the way.

"He called me," I said, still studying my feet. I spotted a green splotch of peas on the toe of my sneaker. At least it wasn't on my shirt.

"Philip? He called you again? When?"

"Just a few minutes ago. He said he was going to make sure you had to leave Atlanta and never had a reason to come back. Noah, Phillip is completely irrational. He thinks you one-upped him all the way through college, and he's determined to make you pay for it now."

"The whole thing is bullshit," Noah said. "It all started our sophomore year, when he went all out to get a grant—a grant he didn't even need—and I ended up getting it. He claimed I stole from him by using a presentation I'd been developing for something else when the grant required original material. But the material *was* original because I never submitted it for the other project. It was a technicality, but I was on the right side of it."

"Is that why he went after every grant you applied for?" I asked.

Noah nodded. "He was determined to beat me. It was so stupid because some of them took a lot of time, and he didn't need the money. It was all ego for him. I was just trying to cover tuition. It didn't help that you and I were together."

"I never even realized he had a thing for me," I said.

"He was quiet about it, but after you and I started dating your freshman year, he shot off his mouth about you, and we got into a fight."

"Which you won. Publicly," I remembered. "Still, he needs to just let it go."

"Yeah, well, he's not doing very well with that."

"I don't think he's going to back off, Noah."

"I don't like him calling you," Noah said.

"Noah, you don't need to worry about me. I made it clear that my loyalty was with you, and Philip didn't take it very well. I don't think he's going to call me again. But he didn't sound like he had any plans to forget about Endicott Tech and leave you alone."

"That's the problem. I need to get back home and talk to some people. This whole thing is unhinged, and part of the reason his accusations have any weight is because he's working for a major social media company. But I've heard some rumors, and so has Dave, that they're not very happy with his vendetta. Normally, I wouldn't go out of my way to get somebody fired but—"

"If that will help shut him down, I think you have to," I said. My stomach twisting and my chest tight, I went on, "I think you should go back to California. And I think we should table this thing with us until you get things settled with Endicott Tech."

Noah shot to his feet, his dark eyes blazing. "What? What does that mean? You're giving up already?"

"I'm not giving up. You're the one who's leaving. And I understand why. It's the right thing to do. But there's no room in your life right now for me. For us. And I can't do this. I can't watch you go, waiting and wondering when you're going to remember I'm here. You have no idea what that was like the first time. I can't do it again. I love you. I've always loved you. And I'm not saying never. I'm just saying not right now. You need to focus on your company. If I'm in the picture, you'll be distracted. I don't want to be a distraction."

The fight drained out of Noah's eyes, and his hands fell to his sides.

"You're not a distraction, Ella. I love you. I know it seems like I'm not focused on us but—"

"How can you be focused on us? Noah, I'm not blaming you. I'm not even mad at you. I just don't want you to string me along again."

"I'm not. I need you to trust me, not run away when things get hard."

"I'm not running away, Noah. I'm trying to protect myself."

"Same thing, Ella. You're not willing to take a risk for us."

"And you are?" I asked. "Tell me you can put me first. Look me in the eyes and tell me that I'm your number one priority."

I waited an agonizing few seconds, but the guilt in his dark eyes was my answer. "You can't. I understand your reasons, but I need to look out for myself, and you need to look out for your company."

Noah looked away, and I headed for the door. I was seconds away from bursting into tears, and I was not doing it in front of Noah.

I was right. He knew I was right.

Leaving him still hurt like hell.

Chapter Ten

Ella

I drove back to Vance and Maggie's through a blur of tears, wiping my eyes as fast as I could so I didn't run off the road. Once I was parked safely in their driveway, I gave in, sobbing until my nose was running and my eyes were red and blotchy.

I've never been a pretty crier. I cleaned myself up as best I could with a baby wipe, stocked in my glovebox thanks to Rosie. I couldn't do anything about my puffy eyes, but at least I didn't have mascara streaked down my cheeks.

I let myself in the front door only forty-five minutes after I'd left, and I heard Vance and Maggie arguing in hushed voices down the hall. I didn't want to interrupt, but I knew better than to look for Rosie without letting them know I was in the house.

Vance and Maggie were older than Holden and Jo, but when it came to messing around, they were just as likely as the younger couple to be caught in a compromising position. After the second time I'd walked in on them, I'd gone for the rudeness of interrupting over being in the house without them knowing.

I walked down the hall to their office, almost stopping when I heard Noah's name.

Maggie said, "Vance, I'm just not comfortable with these allegations. After that lawsuit, it doesn't look good. We have other options, and his software isn't a proven commodity."

"No, and it might never be. But I think the allegations are bullshit. And this Philip guy? I don't trust him at all. Going after Noah like this? It doesn't make Philip look very stable."

"I agree, Philip isn't the issue. But there are people backing him up, and the last thing we want is our name attached to someone who's guilty of stealing intellectual property. We could be liable."

"Not if we can prove we weren't aware of any wrongdoing," Vance countered.

"The damage would be done," Maggie argued. "You're going on your gut here."

"And you're being too practical, sugar."

I didn't have to see Maggie's face to know she was scowling at Vance. She loved to pretend she hated the nickname *Sugar Magnolia*, but I suspected she secretly loved it. I stepped into the doorway of the office, drawing both of their attention.

Before they could speak, I said quietly, "If it helps, I can guarantee that Noah never stole anything from Philip Martin. Not from Philip, and not from anyone else. He's one of the most ethical men I know. When we were in school, he was always voted to lead teams because the other students knew he'd never take credit for their work. Unlike Philip."

"Then why is Philip Martin going after him this way?" Maggie asked. "I know you know Noah better than we do, Ella, but it's also possible that you're not seeing him clearly.

You have a lot of history. And Philip Martin has said some damaging things."

"I know he has. But Philip is a little crazy when it comes to Noah. He always has been. He's had this stupid one-sided competition with Noah since college, always needing to beat him. The more he failed, the more driven he was to even things up."

"That's not rational," Maggie said.

"I know. He called me this afternoon to tell me he was taking care of getting Noah out of Atlanta. I can understand you not wanting to get mixed up in this. And I'm not trying to tell you your business. But if you think Noah is dishonest, I can swear to you that he's not. And if you want to talk to a few people with solid reputations who know him well enough to vouch for him, I'll give you names and numbers. Half the professors at Tech will tell you all you need to know about Noah."

"I've talked to a number of them already," Vance said. "They back you up all the way. He's a leader, ethical, and several of them said—off the record—that there's no way Philip Martin could've come up with the code Noah used to start Endicott Tech. Plus, Philip Martin is an asshole."

"You're not wrong about that," I agreed. "Has he called you?"

"About fifty times. I've only answered twice, but that was more than enough. Noah's coming here at four thirty for a meeting."

Correctly reading my face, Maggie said, "It didn't go well?"

I shook my head. "If I stay upstairs with Rosie when he's here, will you not tell him that I'm around? I don't want to see him right now."

Vance studied me, his sharp blue eyes catching the signs of my tears. "What did he do?"

"Nothing. He didn't do anything." I thought about dinner the night before, the flowers, and the sushi. Noah enrolling me in school and paying my tuition.

He'd done a lot, and all of it was wonderful.

I didn't want to tell Vance and Maggie the details. I hadn't begun to think about how to handle my job with them if I was going back to school.

"He went out of his way to show me how much I mean to him. But his priority has to be his company right now, and coming in second-place is what broke us up the first time. I told him it's over."

"What did he say?" Maggie asked.

"He's not very happy with me. I'd rather not see him before he goes back to California."

Seeming to make some internal decision he didn't share, Vance leaned forward and said, "That's cool. Maggie's got an appointment, and I have to run over to the gallery, but I'll be back by three thirty. We don't need you here for the meeting with Noah. We can handle Rosie. Why don't you plan to head home when I get back?"

"Thank you," I said, relieved. I'd already been through one crying fit today. I could do without another.

Fortunately for me, Rosie was a sweetheart for the rest of the afternoon. When she woke up from her post-lunch nap, I took her and Scout on a long walk that ended in the backyard, where Rosie practiced her walking skills.

Scout, who loved his little mistress even when she wasn't slipping him food, stood beside her, his short legs putting his back at the perfect height for her hand as she took one wobbling step after another.

It blew my mind how much she'd grown since I'd first

started watching her. From barely rolling over and making incoherent baby sounds to walking and talking. I hoped I could figure out a way to go back to school and still work part-time as Rosie's nanny. I couldn't wait to see what the next year would bring.

Watching her leaning into Scout, resting her legs as she stroked his soft ear, I had a flash of another baby, this one with dark hair and bittersweet chocolate eyes. I didn't think of having kids often, but I'd always planned on it. And when I imagined those future babies, they always looked like Noah. Even when we'd been broken up, I hadn't been able to picture a child that wasn't Noah's.

We still had a chance, didn't we? I'd told him we needed to be apart for a while, but not forever. Remembering the look on his face when he told me I was running, I wasn't so sure he agreed.

He would once he had a chance to think things through. He'd get back to California, get sucked into the chaos of Endicott Tech, and realize that I'd been right.

Now wasn't the right time for us. I'd rather let him go than have him forget me again.

When will be the right time?

I didn't want to look ahead, but I couldn't stop myself. If he was too busy for me now, what would happen when the company took off, and they were working like crazy to fill orders and expand? Or if Noah failed and he had to start over? Would he have more time then?

With a sinking heart, I realized there might never be a right time.

Or maybe, the right time was up to us, and I'd just completely messed everything up.

No, I hadn't.

I'd looked Noah in the eyes and asked him if he could

put me first. He hadn't said a word. I wasn't asking him to leave his company. I wasn't even asking him to work less.

I just wanted him to assure me that *we* were a priority.

That we were at least as important as Endicott Technologies.

I could do that for him. I'd always thought of Noah first. I was doing it now, letting him off the hook so he could focus on his dreams for his company.

The only major decision I hadn't made with us in mind was my refusal to leave Tech to follow him to California. But there wouldn't have been anything out there for me. Not like there was in the program with Oliver.

I rescued Scout when Rosie's ear strokes got a little too enthusiastic and resolved to stop thinking about Noah. I was making myself dizzy going in circles of blame. Noah's fault. My fault.

What did it matter?

Either way, we couldn't seem to make it work.

By the time Vance was back and I was ready to leave, Rosie's eyelids were drooping. I changed her and tucked her in before I waved a quick goodbye to Vance and fled.

Noah wasn't due for another hour, but his impending arrival was bearing down on me. I just wanted to get away.

I had done the right thing in cutting him loose. I knew I had. His company was more important to him than anything, and if he was distracted and it slipped through his fingers, a part of him would never forgive me.

Better to say goodbye now so that we could have a chance later. I wouldn't be able to live with myself if he lost his company and I was partially responsible.

Restless and irritable, I didn't want to hang around the loft, but I didn't want to be with people either. I threw on my running clothes, grabbed my headphones, and drove to

Piedmont Park. A slow but exhausting 5K later, I collapsed in my car sweaty but feeling like I'd accomplished something.

I'd only been out of the shower ten minutes when the buzzer at the front door sounded. A quick check of the security camera revealed Holden. I buzzed him up, hoping nothing was wrong. Holden and I were friends, but I didn't think I'd ever hung out with him one on one.

"Hey, what's up?" I asked, trying to sound casual.

He gave me a long stare and said, "You okay?"

"No," I answered, honestly. "I broke things off with Noah. I'm terrible. And I don't want to talk about it."

"Okay, fair enough. I need your help with something," he said.

When he didn't offer any more information, I realized he was a little on edge. Trying to set him at ease, I said, "Do you want a beer? Cup of coffee? I just got back from a run, and I feel like I deserve a beer."

"A beer would be great, thanks," he said.

I pulled out a microbrew I knew Holden would like and opened my own. "So what's going on? What do you need help with?"

"This is a secret."

"I can keep a secret," I promised, suddenly dying of curiosity.

"I want you to go ring shopping with me."

"Oh my God! Oh my God! Seriously? I would love to go ring shopping with you! Oh, I know exactly what she wants." I couldn't help jumping up and down with glee. Then a thought occurred to me. "Wait, not that I'm not flattered, and I *do* know what kind of ring she wants, but why aren't you asking Emily? Jo's one of my best friends, but she and Em are like sisters."

"That's the problem. See—this is part of the secret—Tate is going to propose to Emily, and he wants it to be a surprise. He asked me not to tell Emily that I'm going to propose to Josephine because he's worried that she'll figure it out."

He had a point. Not that Tate and Holden did everything in lockstep, but they'd met their girlfriends, soon to be fiancées, at the same time and had asked them to move in with them, also at the same time. So it wasn't a far stretch for Emily to expect a proposal if she learned that Holden was buying a ring for Jo.

"Sneaky," I said. "You happen to be in luck, because last week, we went out to lunch and decided to do some shopping. We walked by the window of a jewelry store, and they had a display of engagement rings. Jo was pretty clear on which one she liked the best, though I have to warn you, it wasn't cheap."

Not cheap didn't really cover it. We hadn't seen the price tag, but I was familiar with the store, and they didn't carry anything that wasn't the highest of high-end. Besides, just looking at the size of the stone, I could estimate that the price ran in the tens of thousands.

Jo had stared at the ring with wide, covetous eyes. When Emily called her on it, she'd demurred, saying that she didn't need anything like that and she and Holden were happy as they were.

She was lying, but we let her get away with it. No girl wants to be caught admitting how much she wants a proposal that hasn't happened yet. At my comment on the ring's cost, Holden shrugged and grinned.

"WGC has had a good couple of years," he said. That was putting it mildly. *Syndrome*, their flagship game, had made a ton of money, and *Syndrome II* looked like it was going to break those records. "What else am I gonna spend my money on, if not my Josephine? Anyway, she needs a big ring to scare off all the geek boys who pant over her."

"Who are you calling geek boys? You run a gaming company."

"True. But have you seen those guys she works with? I swear they worship the ground she walks on. They follow her around like panting puppies. Nothing I do scares them off. At least Tate has Emily in the office with him. None of our employees would dare to flirt with the boss's girl."

Holden had a point. Jo was the only female on her team, and between her brilliant mind and her bombshell body, the men she worked with were in love. I knew it drove Holden nuts because he'd mentioned it more than once.

"So you're going to buy her a diamond ring to stake your claim?" I asked, laughing. "Maybe you should get her a tattoo on her forehead that says *Property of Holden Winters.*"

He shook his head. "I wouldn't object to tattooing my name on her, but I don't think Josephine would go for it. The ring will have to do. What are you doing Monday? I can sneak out of the office."

"I have to check with Vance and Maggie, but it's probably fine. Worst case, I can bring Rosie in the stroller."

"It's a plan," Holden said, raising his beer in a toast. I clinked the neck of my bottle against his and drank. It was nice to know someone was going to get their happy ending.

Maybe Holden saw the shadow in my eyes because he said, "What happened with Noah?"

"Didn't I say I didn't want to talk about it?" I deflected.

"You did. But sometimes, friends don't listen to other friends when they're making bullshit excuses. Why did you break up with him?"

I tried to explain. I don't think I did a very good job

because when I was done, Holden gave me a long, considering look and shook his head.

"You think he's not going to be distracted without you? It's probably going to be worse. If this is really about keeping his head in the game, you're not helping by taking away the one thing he says he really wants. You."

"But—"

"Unless this is really about protecting yourself," he said, meeting my eyes with a dark stare that somehow reminded me of Noah's.

I set my beer down on the counter. Why was it so wrong to protect myself? Trying to explain, I said, "The last time he left, he got so wrapped up in his company that he completely forgot about me. I don't want to go through that again."

"Fair enough," Holden said. "I can't promise you things are going to work out. He's dealing with a shit-storm right now, and it's a bad time for his company to be in this kind of mess. Philip Martin is a dumbass. He's digging himself a hole, and eventually, he'll get what's coming to him. But here's something to think about—when this is all over, and Noah's life calms down, he's going to remember that you cut him loose when he needed you. He may not want to try again. I get that you want to protect yourself, but is the risk of getting hurt worth losing him?"

Holden drank the rest of his beer, rinsed it out in the sink, and tossed it into the recycle bin.

"Just something to think about." Turning toward the door, he said, "I'll text you on Monday. If Vance and Maggie need you and you can't get away, just let me know. We'll figure it out."

"Sounds good," I said weakly, my head spinning, trying to absorb Holden's parting words.

Was that how Noah saw it? Me cutting him loose? Abandoning him?

Was that what I was doing?

Lost in thought, I followed Holden downstairs and locked the door behind him when he left.

Gradually, it dawned on me that I'd made a terrible mistake.

CHAPTER ELEVEN
NOAH

I had a bad feeling about the meeting with Vance and Maggie Winters. Vance had been abrupt on the phone that afternoon, demanding that I make time to stop by before I headed to the airport. I had time. My flight wasn't until almost eleven pm. I never had trouble sleeping on a plane, even squeezed into coach, and I preferred not to waste the day sleeping when I could do it while I flew. I'd planned to take Ella to dinner, but it looked like that wasn't going to happen.

I was trying not to think about Ella. I couldn't say I was surprised she'd ended things. Hell, we'd barely gotten back together before she lost her nerve and walked. Maybe it was for the best. A long-distance relationship wouldn't be easy. If she couldn't trust me, it would fall apart, just as it had before.

I was trapped, and I couldn't figure my way out. I couldn't walk away from my company. Not only was it the product of years of hard work, but my team was counting on me. Even if I didn't want to run the company anymore, I couldn't let it fail. If I really wanted to move on, we had to finish this project and get it on the market. Then I could sell the company and start over with something else. Something with less stress. I could get a regular job.

Would Ella give me a shot if I had a regular job with none of the demands of running my own company? My stomach twisted at the thought. What if I sold the company and she did come back?

That guy wasn't me.

I'd been dreaming of Endicott Tech the whole time we were together. A regular nine to five was never on my radar. If that's the man she wanted, I was better off without her. I felt sick as that realization crystallized in my mind.

Endicott Technologies was a part of me. It was who I was. I'd never be happy with less than my own dream. If less was what Ella wanted, then as much as I loved her, I was better off without her.

I parked my car in Vance and Maggie's driveway, queasy at the thoughts rolling in my brain. Was I giving up on Ella?

No, I refused to give up.

She hadn't asked me to sell Endicott Tech. She'd said she was breaking things off so I could focus on work. She didn't want me to change. She just didn't think there was room for her in my dream.

Frustration coursed through me as I got out of my rental car and paced to the front door. I didn't want to be here dealing with business. I needed to spend my last hours in Atlanta talking to Ella. There was more to say—she just didn't know it yet.

Maggie swung open the door with a smile, little Rosie balanced on her hip, tugging on Maggie's long red hair. "Come in, Noah. Vance is in the office." She gestured down the hall.

"Aren't you coming?" I asked. Maggie had been an integral part of every meeting and conference call we'd had so far. If she wasn't joining us, it couldn't mean good things.

She shook her head, gently tugging her hair free from her daughter's tight fist. "I'm out. Vance and I aren't seeing eye to eye. But Noah? I like you. I'm more cautious than Vance, and I'm not happy about this mess with Phillip Martin, but I like you. I hope you make the right choice."

With that oblique comment, she walked away, singing a nursery rhyme under her breath, Rosie trying to sing along with limited success. I watched them go, thinking about family, and children, and Ella. Whenever I imagined those things, which admittedly wasn't often, it was with Ella.

Always Ella.

Even when we were apart, she was the woman I thought of when I thought of forever.

Resolved to get this meeting over with, I strode down the hall to the office. Vance sat at his desk, working on his laptop. He looked up when I knocked on the open door. With his hair pulled back in a low ponytail, wearing a faded t-shirt and torn jeans, his tattoos dark lines on his tanned skin, he looked every inch the artist and nothing like a savvy investor.

"Noah, take a seat," he said, nodding to the chair opposite him. I did, trying not to let his hard blue gaze disconcert me. "I've got an offer for you."

"Am I going to like it?" I asked.

Vance shot me a sharp grin. "I don't know. Why don't we find out? Take a look."

He slid me a few sheets of paper, a revision of the deal we'd been discussing for weeks. Everything looked good. Their buy-in was generous. They'd get a stake in the company but wouldn't be able to take control from me. It was everything we'd been talking about. Exactly what I'd been working for. With this money, I'd be able to keep the company going until we had the new product ready for the market. We'd be in the clear.

Relief speared through me; then it dissolved when Vance said, "There's a condition."

Of course, there was. After all the damage Phillip had done, this deal was too good to be true. "What's the condition?"

"You agree never to contact Ella again."

That was the last thing I was expecting. A penalty for delays on getting to market, sure. Higher ownership stake if we needed a second infusion of cash, maybe. But turning my back on Ella? That didn't make any sense.

"Are you serious?" I finally asked.

"Dead serious. You need to focus on your company. And Ella is like family. She's been working with Maggie and me, taking care of Rosie for six months. She's close to Holden and Tate, as well as Jo and Emily. She's more than an employee. We care about her. And you're making her miserable. I'm looking out for her. You back off, don't see her again, and we'll give you everything you need to make Endicott Tech a success. You call her, try to see her, and we're out."

"What if I take the deal and then decide I want Ella?" I asked, trying to see the deal from all the angles. I wanted this money, but I wanted Ella, too. If there were any way I could have both . . . I had to figure it out.

"We'll draw up a clause that allows us to pull out, with penalties, if you have contact with her. At any time."

"And if she calls me?" I asked.

"She won't," Vance said. "You've already let her go twice. She's not going to come back for a third time. Take the money and forget about Ella. You can have everything you've ever wanted." Vance shrugged a shoulder in dismissal. "There are other girls in California. You need your company more than you need her."

I stared at Vance with blind eyes, his words a jumble in my mind.

I wanted that money for the company. I needed Ella for me.

You can have everything you've ever wanted.

No, I couldn't. Not if I couldn't have Ella.

I imagined saying yes. Going back to California. Getting the product out on the market. Making my team's dreams come true. Instead of anticipation, it all felt flat. Empty. I hadn't had Ella before, but somewhere in the back of my mind, I'd always planned to reconnect with her. I'd always assumed we'd find a way to be together. Without Ella, without the hope of someday being with her, nothing else mattered.

There were other girls in California, but I didn't want another girl. I wanted Ella. My Ella.

I'd been shying away from investing my savings in Endicott Tech. I'd worked my ass off for every penny. Having a safety net helped me sleep at night. But without Vance, I could still pull this off. Fuck getting investors. I'd sell my house, sell my cars. I'd drain my savings if that's what it took to save Endicott Tech on my own terms.

It wasn't the best business decision, but if I went my own way, I could do right by my company and still go after Ella. I wasn't letting her walk away from me. Not this time.

"No thanks," I said, shoving the papers back in Vance's hand. His eyebrows shot up in surprise.

"Are you sure? You won't get a deal like this from anyone else."

"I know. I don't care. I'll do this on my own if I have to. Thanks for your time."

I was striding to the front door when I heard Vance call out, a laugh in his voice, "Good luck!"

Asshole.

I checked my phone. 4:45pm. Ella should be home. If she wasn't, I was going to track her down. I wasn't leaving Atlanta until we'd worked things out.

My phone rang just as I was parking my car a block from her front door.

Ella.

I answered, breathless with sudden nerves. "Ella?"

"Noah! Where are you? Have you left yet?" Her voice was thin and fast, like she was running.

"I'm almost at your front door," I said.

The door swung open to reveal Ella, wearing loose-fitting cotton pajama pants and a red tank top, her dark hair wet and pulled back from her face with a clip.

"I was just going to look for you," she said. I noticed her keys clutched in one hand.

Raising an eyebrow, I asked, "In that?"

She looked down at herself and flushed, slowly shaking her head. "I realized I needed to see you and I forgot what I was wearing."

"Can I come in?"

"Yes. Please come in." I followed her to the elevator, unable to take my eyes off her. She was jittery, her breath coming too fast, flags of pink in her cheeks.

"Why were you looking for me?" I asked.

Ella set her phone and keys on the kitchen island and turned to look at me. Taking a deep breath to steady herself, she said, "I'm sorry about everything I said earlier. You were right; I was running away because I don't want to get hurt again. I'm scared. But I want to try. I don't want to give up on us."

I thought about telling her how things had worked out with Vance and Maggie. In theory, giving up all that money for her should prove how serious I was. But I didn't want her to know. I didn't want her to be with me because of a big gesture.

Anyone could make a big gesture. Big gestures were a one-time thing. Trust took more than that. Trust was day-to-day. Trust was the little things. If this was going to work, we needed the time to build that.

Taking a step toward her, I took her hands in mine. "Ella, I love you. I know this isn't going to be easy. You've got at least a year of school ahead of you, and we both know I have a problem with getting sucked into work."

Ella let out an uneasy laugh. "I'm going to try to be more understanding about that, Noah. I know how important your company is to you."

"Not as important as you. I promise. Nothing is more important than you."

She looked up at me, her dark eyes serious as she framed my face with her hands. Drawing me down, she pressed her soft lips to mine. "I'm sorry I got scared," she said against my mouth.

"I'm sorry the timing is so fucked up."

I kissed her, pulling her body into mine and slanting my mouth over hers. She was mine. We were going to do this together. I kissed her until she was liquid heat in my arms, until the clothes between us were too much distance. Her lips swollen, Ella tipped her head back, studying me as if she wanted to memorize every nuance of my face.

"You have to go, don't you?" she asked, dropping her head to rest on my shoulder.

I did. I couldn't bring myself to say it. Instead, I said, "Not yet. I have a little time."

Looking up at me with a glint in her eye, Ella asked, "How much time?"

"A few hours."

"Do you want to talk?" she asked coyly.

I scooped her up and tossed her over my shoulder, striding toward her bedroom.

"We can talk on the phone."

I tossed her on her bed, stripping her loose cotton pajama pants down her legs. I had my own clothes off seconds later. I was already peeling Ella's tank top up to reveal her gorgeous breasts and perfect, hard, pink nipples . . . when reality interrupted.

Condom.

Fuck.

Praying I still had one in my wallet, I dove off the side of the bed and snagged my jeans, yanking out my wallet and flipping through.

Jackpot.

Ella watched me, her eyebrows knit together, teeth sunk into her lower lip. When she saw the red plastic square in my hand, her expression cleared, the frown replaced with a saucy grin.

"I'll make a doctor appointment and go on the pill or something."

"Whatever you want, Els. I'll get tested, so you know you don't have to worry." I didn't ask her for the same. I already knew no one had touched her in the last two years but me. Not for the first time, I wished I could say the same.

I couldn't decide where I wanted to start. Ella's body stretched across the bed was a buffet of delights. If we had more time, if I weren't leaving in a matter of hours, I might have made a different choice. But this time, the last time I'd to touch her for at least a few weeks, maybe more, I wanted intimacy more than anything else.

I stretched out beside her, pulling her into my arms and kissing her. I could kiss Ella all day. Her mouth fit mine as if she'd been made for me. Every part of her was mine—the sounds she made in the back of her throat, the way her body moved into mine as our kiss grew deeper. Nothing, no woman, had ever been like this. Ella was magic. And she was mine.

When I thought I would go mad from not being inside her, I drew back to open the condom and rolled it down my desperately hard cock. The look in her eyes as she watched me, the heat and the hunger, was almost too much. I rolled to my back and pulled her on top of me.

"Like this," I said. "I want to watch you."

If I had to pick a favorite position with Ella, this had to be it. Watching her as she rode me, seeing the passion on her face, the way her skin flushed as she drew closer and closer to orgasm, the sway of her breasts, the curve of her hips. I loved how easy it was to draw her down and suck her nipples, how easy it was to kiss her.

She straddled me, rising above me, and trailed her fingers up the length of my cock before stroking the head over her pussy, front to back, rubbing gentle circles over her clit.

Fuck. Watching the woman I loved pleasure herself with my body was fucking hot. I couldn't resist reaching out to slide a finger inside her. Yeah, she was teasing me. Her pussy was slick and ready. I withdrew my finger and ran my hands up the sides of her thighs, rocking my hips up a few inches, teasing her back. Her eyelids drooped, and her breath hitched in her chest.

Leaning forward, she set the head of my cock against her pussy and slowly, inch by inch, lowered her body onto mine. My eyes wanted to roll up into the back of my head, but I kept them open, focused on Ella's face, watching bliss spread across her features as I filled her.

She started rocking above me slowly, getting used to the stretch of me inside her, cupping her breasts with her hands and tugging on her nipples in a way she knew would drive me crazy.

It did.

Usually, when she was on top, part of the game was to hold myself back until I couldn't take it anymore. Letting her tease me until we were both insane with need added an edge to the sweetness of watching her ride me to orgasm.

It had been too long, and I couldn't play. When she started making the little moans that told me she was close, I pulled her down, took her mouth with mine, and rolled us over.

Kissing her, driving my cock into her over and over, it wasn't long before she arched her back beneath me and let out a low, gasping wail. I followed her into orgasm, for a fleeting moment wishing the condom weren't between us, wishing I was filling her with me.

When I had my breath back and thought I could walk without wobbling, I went to the bathroom to take care of the condom. When I came back, Ella was still in bed, the sheet pulled up, her face drowsy and a tiny smile of satisfaction on her lips.

"You look pleased with yourself," I commented as I slid into bed beside her. I still had an hour or two before I had to leave for the airport, and I didn't want to waste a minute of it.

"I *am* very pleased with myself," she said, rolling to face me. She lifted her hand and traced her fingers down the side of my face, from my temple to my chin. "We can do this, Noah. We have to promise to be honest with each other, to tell each other if we feel like it's not working so we can figure out a way around our problems instead of just getting angry and giving up."

"You mean, you want to debug our relationship?"

She laughed. Even when we were fighting, we always understood each other. "Exactly. Last time, I was hurt you weren't calling, and then you didn't show up for graduation. I reacted emotionally when I told you it was over. I don't want to do that again. I know you're going to get distracted with work, even though you won't mean to. When I go back to school, the same will probably happen to me. I don't want either of us sitting on opposite sides of the country thinking the other one doesn't care. When things start getting hard, we need to talk about it. Figure out where we're going wrong and what we can do differently. Just like we would with a buggy program."

"Have I ever told you you're brilliant?" I asked. Maybe to someone else, Ella's debug approach to relationship troubles would sound insane. Not to me.

"A few times," she said. "Did you work things out with Vance and Maggie?"

"No. They had some conditions that didn't work for me. I'm going to do this myself."

"I thought you said that was bad business," she pointed out. I hoped I could distract her because I didn't want to explain how things had gone down with Vance. Personally, I thought her employer was a dick, but I knew Ella adored Vance and Maggie, and they'd been good to her. Better than good.

Vance was right—they treated her like she was family. If

I told her Vance's condition, she'd probably be angry with him, and she didn't need that complication in her life right now. The issues with the company were my problem. I wasn't going to drag Ella in the middle.

"It *is* bad business, in a way. I'm going to see about getting a mortgage on my house when I get back. I thought about selling it, but if word gets out I'm selling my house, it will undermine faith in Endicott Tech. I bought it for cash back when I had a ton of it and was looking to invest. I should be able to get a lot of equity on it. Interest rates are low, so it won't be too bad. And I have a few cars I bought for fun and never drive that I could do without. Some other stuff like that. I'll see what I can do to raise enough money to get us through the next few months. If that's not good enough, there's always my savings."

"Noah, that sounds risky."

"It is. If this goes the wrong way, if we take too long to get the product out, I could end up with close to nothing. I could lose the company. Are you okay with that?"

"Noah, I don't care about money. I appreciate that you paid my tuition. It means so much. But I know how to work hard. So do you. Even if I don't finish grad school, we both have marketable skills. We'll be okay. I'm not in love with Silicon Valley's newest tech billionaire. I'm in love with you. I loved you when we were both doing work-study and hustling for scholarships and grants. If you lose everything tomorrow, I'll still love you. I'll always love you. Do what you need to do with the company. Follow your gut. I'll be by your side, even if it's from across the country."

"I love you, Els."

We lay there for another forty minutes, whispering about nothing and everything until an alarm beeped on my phone, reminding me that I needed to get moving if I didn't want to miss my flight.

Ella made me a sandwich while I took a quick shower. She walked me to the door, waving me off with a smile and her dark eyes filled with tears and hope.

I'd come to Atlanta hoping to score a deal for my company and reconnect with Ella. The deal was history, but I had Ella back, and she loved me.

No business deal, no company, was as important as Ella. As long as I had her, we would figure the rest out. Together.

Epilogue
Ella

"I do."

The officiant barely got out the words, "I now pronounce you husband and wife. You may kiss the bride," before Tate scooped Emily into his arms, bent her back, and laid a kiss on her mouth that was borderline inappropriate for a wedding.

I don't think Emily minded.

I hadn't been to many weddings, and this one was so small it was more like a family get-together than a formal event, but I knew I wouldn't attend many that were sweeter or more perfect for the bride and groom.

Despite the short timeframe between proposal and wedding, Emily had found a dress that suited her perfectly, sleek, modern, and stylish, just like Emily herself. The dress modestly draped her curves while still being sexy as hell, and she glowed in the white satin, her dark hair pinned into an elaborate coronet of braids and twists, her gray eyes luminous.

Tate wore the standard tux in a deep charcoal gray, his blue eyes bright with happiness and his dark hair a little too long. When he'd said he'd get it cut for the wedding, Emily had demanded he leave it.

Only Holden and Jo stood up with them. As Tate knew she would, Emily had wanted a small, private ceremony. Aside from me, another friend we'd gone to school with, and Sophie, their aunt Amelia's nurse, the wedding guests were all Winters. That said, they were a big family, and we easily filled the formal dining room.

It was a lovely evening and a perfect way to celebrate New Year's day, watching two people I adored pledge their hearts to one another surrounded by friends. The fantastic food and decadent surroundings didn't hurt.

Still, I missed Noah. I hadn't seen him since the beginning of December when I'd taken a week off and flown out to California. He'd been working for some of that time, but he'd taken off as much as he could, and we'd spent a blissful week together.

I liked California. I liked where he lived, right down to the neighborhood. I'd told him I'd love him if he had nothing, and I meant it. If Noah came to me naked and penniless, he would still be my dream man. After seeing his house, though, I was hoping he pulled off his gamble and was able to keep it because it was spectacular.

I hadn't been sure how he expected a mortgage on a house to keep his company going since I'd been under the impression he needed a lot of cash. I'd forgotten that real estate in Northern California isn't cheap, and his modern, custom-built home in the woods with its soaring ceilings, plate glass windows, and the best of everything, designed by a renowned architect, was worth a fortune. Let's just say the equity he pulled out of the house set him up for a while.

If he had to sell it, he'd walk away with nothing, and

we'd deal. But if he could keep it, I'd be more than happy living there.

So far, he was optimistic. Their software was almost ready for the market. Actually, a lot of companies would have released it already, bugs and all. The pressure to ship software was so intense that most companies released well before they'd worked out all the issues. With the stigma of Philip Martin's accusations hanging over Endicott Technologies, Noah didn't want to risk shipping a product that wasn't perfect, or as close as they could reasonably get it.

Philip was out of the picture. He'd continued to make trouble for a few weeks after Noah had returned to California. The planned protest had gone off, complete with picketers outside Endicott Tech's corporate offices. When a popular tech blog exposed those picketers as actors, Philip went from righteous vigilante to laughingstock.

The last we'd heard, shortly before Christmas, he'd lost his job. We were prepared for him to come at Noah again, but his reputation had been damaged so much, his threats would carry far less weight.

It wasn't until after Thanksgiving that I found out what had happened between Vance and Noah. Noah had refused to say a word, only telling me that Vance had conditions he wasn't willing to satisfy.

When I'd asked for the week off to visit Noah, Vance had said, "I didn't expect him to take the deal, you know. I hoped he wouldn't, but I had to offer."

"What deal?" I'd asked, confused.

One of Vance's blonde eyebrows shot up. "He didn't tell you?"

"All he said was that he didn't like your conditions and he was going to do it on his own. He mortgaged as much of his house as the bank would let him and sold as many things that he thought he could without drawing attention."

"Interesting. I wonder if he's still open to an investment. Without the conditions."

Suspicious, I asked, "What were the conditions?"

Vance refused to tell me. So did Noah.

Noah said it was between him and Vance, and everything had turned out for the best. Maggie stepped in and tried to salvage the deal, but Noah had politely turned her down. He'd made her a counter-offer—once he had a guarantee of a viable product and a solid timeline, they'd need cash for production and expansion.

Endicott Technologies wasn't going to license or sell the software they'd developed. They wanted to produce and distribute it in-house, including the hardware to run it. That was going to take money Noah couldn't raise through mortgages and selling cars. Especially since he'd already mortgaged his house and sold his cars.

Maggie and Vance had been satisfied by his counter-offer of future business, but I'd heard her giving Vance a hard time over the way he'd interfered between Noah and me. After that, I was determined to find out what had really happened.

Maggie was good at keeping secrets, but she had a low tolerance to alcohol. I dragged it out of her one night after she'd had one too many glasses of wine. When I learned the truth, I'd started to cry.

I knew Noah loved me.

I did.

Learning that he'd risked his company, that he'd chosen me over Endicott Technologies and then hadn't used it as leverage to win me back . . .

Understanding what he'd put on the line for me made me dizzy with love. I never told him I knew.

"Another glass of wine?" A waiter in a white dinner jacket asked, offering a bottle of red.

"No, thank you," I said.

From beside me, Jo said, "You can stay here tonight, you know."

"I know, and I appreciate it, but I think I'm all partied out."

Jo gave me a knowing look and shared a glance with Holden. They both knew that as much as I'd loved the wedding, I was a little down. Noah was supposed to be in Atlanta for New Year's Eve, the night before, but there was a massive weather system in the Midwest dumping snow and ice everywhere, and almost every flight in the country had been delayed or rerouted. Nothing was running on time.

Instead of flying straight from Northern California to Atlanta, Noah had been hopscotching the country trying to get here. The last I heard, he was in Houston, grounded due to ice. He was doing everything he could to get here, and I knew I'd see him soon, but being at the wedding without him was a disappointment.

Not just for me. I hated thinking about him spending the New Year's holiday alone in a strange airport.

"He'll get here," she reassured me, giving my hand a squeeze. I couldn't help but notice the ring on her finger, the exact one she'd seen that day with Emily and me, the same ring I'd pointed out to Holden. Once he'd bought it and Tate had safely whisked Emily out of town for a romantic weekend and surprise proposal, Holden had wasted no time in sliding it onto Josephine's finger. It looked perfect there.

I'd caught Jo staring at it with a happy smile more than a

few times since Holden had asked her to be his wife. Unlike Emily, Jo wanted a traditional wedding. Nothing huge like the wedding Holden's older brother, Jacob, was planning, but bigger than both of the weddings the Winters family had thrown in the last two weeks.

According to Jo and Em, Winters House had been a whirlwind between Charlotte Winters's wedding to Lucas Jackson on Christmas Eve and then Em and Tate's much smaller ceremony today.

Raised voices at the other end of the table had me sitting up straighter. Both Holden and Jo leaned forward, trying to see what was going on. A low voice swore loudly, followed by the crash of silverware.

"Oh, shit," Holden said, glancing my way. "I apologize in advance for my family."

"What's going on?" I asked.

Jo shook her head as Holden said, "Aiden and Gage have some shit to work out." Craning his neck to see past his cousin Vance, he said, "Here it comes."

A second later, the meaty thud of a fist hitting flesh sounded, followed by a roar of rage. I smacked my hand over my mouth, watching in awe as Holden's refined, austere older brother, Aiden, launched himself at his cousin Gage, taking the former special forces soldier to the carpet in a whirlwind of writhing limbs and swinging fists.

"Oh, my God!" Jo whispered to me. "I would have bet my engagement ring Aiden wouldn't be the one to start a brawl in his own dining room."

"Technically, Gage started it," Holden said, taking a sip of wine and watching the fight. He made no effort to hide his amusement. None of them did. Tate was outright grinning.

"Aren't any of you going to stop it?" I asked. As if she'd

144

heard me, Aunt Amelia's nurse, Sophie, jumped to her feet. She stormed over to the men and stared down at them with her hands on her hips. Just when I thought she was going to do something to stop the fight, she turned on her heel and left the room, muttering under her breath something about men and idiots.

Answering my question, Holden said, "Nope. I'm not getting in the middle of those two. A guy could get hurt that way."

"Holden—" Jo protested.

"They'll be done soon," he assured us. "This has been brewing for years. They'll both feel better after they pound on each other for a while."

The fight showed no signs of stopping. Both men were on the ground, and they looked so much alike it was hard to see who was winning. Holden and the other Winters boys might be fine with watching their two oldest battle it out in the formal dining room, but I was feeling distinctly out of place.

Carrie, our friend from school, was sitting to my left. She leaned in and said quietly, "Are they usually like this?"

"No idea," I whispered back.

"I'm kind of feeling like it's time to head out," she said.

I had to agree. The fight showed no signs of slowing down. If they didn't stop soon, someone was going to get hurt. From across the table, I heard a female voice say, "If he bleeds on the carpet, Mrs. W is going to be pissed."

If someone was bleeding, it was definitely time to go. Sending a wave across the table to the bride and groom, I leaned over to hug Jo and said, "Carrie and I are out of here. Call you later."

Fortunately, the brawl was far enough from the door that we could slip out mostly unnoticed. The Winters family didn't do anything low-profile. Even a small family wedding had turned into a circus. I loved them all to pieces, but I preferred my simple life to their drama and scandal-filled existence.

All I needed was Noah and school.

I couldn't help checking my phone before starting the car. It remained stubbornly dark and silent. No word from Noah. The weather was easing in the Northeast and upper Midwest, but ice storms were scattered across the South and Southwest, exactly where Noah was the last time he'd texted.

I wanted him at my side, but more, I wanted him safe. I tried to banish the image of him sitting on the floor in an airport terminal, propping his head on his briefcase while he tried to catch a nap. Ever since I'd seen news coverage of the flight delays, seen hundreds of people in that exact position over the holiday, the idea of Noah alone and far from me had been driving me nuts.

The weather wasn't great in Atlanta, but the streets were mostly clear of ice and the night had remained blessedly dry. I drove Carrie home cautiously, waiting outside her apartment building until she was safe in the lobby. I don't know what I expected as I drove back to the loft. Noah's car parked out front? Noah waiting on my doorstep? Either way, I was disappointed.

I was still living in the loft, though Noah's tuition payment had included money for room and board. Vance, overprotective and suspicious, had insisted that I continue living in the loft just in case. I'd tried to argue, but Maggie shook her head and advised me to just give in, saying that unless I had a compelling reason to live in student housing, the loft was far more comfortable and it would get Vance off my back.

Vance and Maggie hadn't wanted to let me go when I started school, and I hadn't wanted to quit. For the first semester, most of my obligations were later in the afternoon, so we'd agreed that I'd continue helping them out in the mornings as well as the occasional evening and weekend, and we'd see how it went.

I loved working for Vance and Maggie and adored little Rosie, and I needed a way to earn money while I was in school. I wasn't taking living expenses from Noah. Not when things were stretched so tight for him. He'd already paid my tuition. That was more than enough.

I stripped off my cocktail dress, let down my hair, and crawled into bed, hoping I'd have news from Noah by morning.

An insistent buzzing woke me from a deep sleep. I rolled over and sat up, squinting into the darkness, trying to make sense of the obnoxious sound filling the loft.

The door!

I lurched out of bed in the dark, half-tripping over a pair of shoes I'd left on the floor, and raced for the video screen by the elevator. Clicking the button to bring it to life, my heart leaped in my chest.

Noah. He looked exhausted and wet, but it was Noah. I hit the button to unlock the door and jumped into the freight elevator. When the doors opened on the first level, he was there.

I threw myself into his arms, planting kisses everywhere I could reach—his forehead, his cheeks, his neck, his collarbone, his lips. My mouth moved over his skin as I murmured his name, *Noah, Noah, Noah.*

Finally, I pulled back to ask, "How did you get here?"

His arms closed around me, holding me tightly as he

dropped his head and took a deep breath. Exhaling, he stepped back and looked down at me.

"You don't want to know. Let's just say I had to promise our firstborn to get a rental car and the roads are a fucking mess."

Belatedly, I realized not only was he wet, but he was freezing cold. More icy rain. Reaching up to brush his damp hair off his face, I said, "Were you out there driving in this? Noah! What if you'd been in an accident?"

"I wasn't. And I'm here. It took me three days, but I'm here." Backing me into the elevator, he pressed the button to take us to the second floor and eyed me from head to toe, taking in my flushed cheeks, my tangled hair, and my night-gown, a barely-there navy blue silk slip. "You normally answer the door dressed like that?" he asked.

"Only when it's you."

I twined my fingers with his, alarmed at how cold they were. "You drove here? Didn't your car have heat?"

He shrugged. "It was supposed to."

I dragged him into the bedroom, darted into the bath-room to start a hot shower, and returned to find him standing there, his bag on the floor beside him as he tried to toe off his shoes. Watching him fumble, I realized how exhausted he must be. I needed to get him warmed up and in bed. By the time I'd peeled off his wet clothes, steam billowed from the shower.

For a second, I thought about letting him go in by himself, but when his fingers closed over my wrist, and he gave a tug, I happily followed. My silk slip only got a little wet before I stripped it over my head and tossed it to the bathroom floor. Noah stood under the hot water, letting it beat down on him, gradually relaxing under the warming spray. I poured body wash into my hands and smoothed it over his skin, taking my time as I explored every inch of the body I knew so well and had missed so much.

I knew Noah was feeling better when he filled his own hands with soap and went to work on me. He took his time, exploring every inch of my body, and when he was done, I was a quivering, aroused mess, desperate for more.

So was Noah. I'd been on the pill since the middle of November, so we didn't have to worry about condoms anymore. Thank God. I didn't want anything between us when he lifted me, pinning my back to the tile wall of the shower and thrusting inside.

A month without Noah felt like a lifetime. We were doing well with the distance thing, learning patience and understanding, but nothing felt as good as being right here.

Noah surrounding me.

Noah filling me.

Noah everywhere.

Dropping his head until his lips grazed my ear, he said in a ragged voice, "Ella, Ella, I can't wait, baby. It's been so long."

I was right there with him, already on the edge of orgasm. I could barely get my head together enough to talk, but I whispered, "Don't wait, don't wait, Noah. I want to feel you come."

Turning my head, I kissed the side of his jaw and nipped his full lower lip. Against his mouth, I said, "Fuck me hard and come inside me, Noah."

He did exactly that, his deep, hard thrusts grinding the base of his cock into my clit and driving me over the edge. My body clamped down on his as I cried out his name.

It was a minute or two before we got our breath back and he set me on my feet. My knees wobbled, and I fell into his chest, knowing his arms would come around me, holding me up.

"Welcome home," I said.

Noah's thorough kiss was answer enough. We let the water rinse us clean, then Noah shut it off and dried me, squeezing the moisture out of my hair and stroking the towel over my skin. He dried himself with brusque strokes, watching with heavily lidded eyes as I braided my damp hair so I wouldn't wake up with a tangled bird's nest on my head.

"Are you hungry?" I asked.

"I can wait till morning. I got drive-through after I hit the road. I just want to go to bed with you."

That, I could do. Taking his hand, I led him to the bed. Before he joined me, he unzipped his bag and pulled something out, hiding it behind his back.

When we were securely tucked beneath the covers, on our sides and facing one another, Noah said, "I've got something for you."

He handed me a black velvet box. I looked from the box to him, confused. Was it a Christmas present? Knowing we'd be together over New Year's, we hadn't exchanged gifts yet. It looked like jewelry, but I didn't want to read anything into it.

Taking the box with fingers that suddenly felt stiff and unwieldy, I pried open the lid. And stared.

It wasn't just jewelry—it was a ring. And not just any ring. It was a perfect diamond solitaire in a classic six-prong platinum setting.

It was an engagement ring.

But Noah hadn't proposed.

Unless this was his idea of a proposal. Uncertain, I pried my eyes from the ring and met Noah's bittersweet chocolate gaze. There was a line between his eyebrows when he said, "I know it's too soon. You don't have to see it as an engagement ring if it's too much. It can just be a promise. A promise that when you're finished with school and we can be together every day, there's going to be an engagement, and we're going to get married."

"So this isn't an engagement ring?"

"Do you want it to be? I tried to talk myself into waiting until you're done with school, or we've had more time. But I know what I want, Ella. I know *who* I want. There's never been another woman I've imagined as my wife. There's never been anyone I dreamed of spending my life with except you. I've loved you since the first day you sat beside me in class and asked to borrow my pen. If you're not ready to be engaged, I'll wait, but I want you to keep the ring. And when we're apart for too long, and life is crazy, I want you to look at that ring and know that you carry my love with you all the time, not just in your heart but on your hand."

A tear trickled from the corner of my eye. Maybe it *was* too soon. We'd barely been back together for two months. But *I* knew what *I* wanted, too.

Noah.

Always Noah.

I pulled that gorgeous, perfect ring from the box and handed it to Noah. "Put it on my finger," I said. "It's not a promise ring. It's an engagement ring."

Noah slid the ring on my finger, then he pulled my hand to his lips and kissed it.

"I want to wait until I finish school for the wedding," I said. "I don't want to be your wife until we're done with living apart."

"Agreed."

Noah grinned at me, his dark eyes shining. "I love you,

Els. The second you finish school, we're getting married. I don't care if it's a big wedding or a small one. I don't care where it is as long as when it's done, I get to go home with you."

That was the kind of deal I could live with. Noah tossed the velvet box over the side of the bed and pulled me into his arms, arranging me so my head was pillowed on his shoulder, my left hand on his chest, his fingers twined with mine, the ring sparkling in the dim light of the bedroom.

I knew exactly what Noah meant when he said it was a promise ring. We were engaged to be married, but that ring was a promise that neither of us would ever forget what we'd learned.

Nothing is more important than love. Nothing. Though I didn't need the ring to remind me. Not as long as I had Noah.

Sneak Peek
The Billionaire's Angel

Chapter One: Sophie

My hands shook as I measured a short length of tape. Staring down at the black cockroach in my hand, I wondered again how I'd gotten myself into this mess.

It's not what you're thinking. The cockroach wasn't real. I've learned how to be brave in the past few years, but not brave enough to carry around live bugs. Yuck. No, this cockroach had been carefully cut out of black construction paper, along with the selection of spiders and crickets spread across the seat of the leather couch.

It was after two in the morning and I was in my employer's library, fumbling in the dark to tape the fake bugs to the inside of the white silk lampshades. The next person to flip on the lights would be treated to the illusion that huge bugs lurked inside the lamps. I could already imagine the screams that would echo through the house. It wouldn't be the first time.

I really had to find a way to keep my charge off the

internet. Boredom plus an active mind equals trouble. At least it does when your name is Amelia Winters.

Since Amelia was seventy-eight and her hands weren't as nimble as mine, I got roped into carrying out the pranks she dreamed up. I was supposed to be her nurse, and I was, when she needed one.

High blood pressure and type two diabetes meant she needed some supervision, but not enough to require live in care. Since most of the family had moved out of the enormous house, and Amelia's great nephew Aiden traveled often for work, I was there to keep her both healthy and entertained.

It could have been a lonely job, if not for Amelia. Her pranks aside, she was a blast to work for - funny and loyal and sweet. Her body was slowing down, but her mind was sharp and she had a wicked sense of humor. Sometimes too wicked.

The pranks, case in point. At least once a week she came up with a new one, sending me out for materials and instructing me on the details of her plans.

At first, I'd worried she was going to get me fired. Since my husband had died I'd been bouncing from job to job. I'd been more than ready to settle down when I'd been hired here and I hadn't wanted to be kicked out for lining the hallway with tiny cups filled with water.

Amelia might be almost eighty, but her sense of humor was a lot more frat-boy than elderly matron.

Fortunately for me, the family was well versed in Amelia's ways. Aiden, who'd scared the heck out of me when he'd hired me, adored his great-aunt. She could probably set the house on fire and he'd laugh and kiss her on the cheek. The rest of them were the same, affectionate and amused by Amelia's antics. The only two exceptions were the housekeeper, Mrs. Williamson, and Aiden's cousin, Gage.

Mrs. Williamson and Amelia were chalk and cheese. Mrs. W was far too proper to admit she didn't love *every* member of the Winters family, but we all knew Amelia drove her nuts. Amelia, for her part, delighted in pestering Mrs. W. More than once I'd heard her mutter under her breath that Mrs. W had a stick up her you know where.

She'd never say it, but I'm pretty sure Mrs. W thought Amelia should give in and act her age. I'd only been with the family for six months, but I could have told her that was a lost cause. By all accounts Amelia Winters had never acted her age and at seventy-eight, she wasn't about to start.

I adored Amelia, and I had to admit, some of her pranks were funny, but I liked Mrs. W too much to let her think her beloved Winters House was infested with six-inch cockroaches. As soon as I'd taped the last fake insect in place, I pulled out my phone to shoot Mrs. W a warning text.

Sometime tomorrow she'd come into the library on a made-up pretext and let out a very convincing scream. Amelia would get her laugh, and Mrs. W wouldn't have to kill her. Everyone would be happy.

I tapped SEND on my text and went to shove the phone in the pocket of my robe when two arms closed around my chest like steel bars, pinning my arms to my sides.

My phone tumbled from nerveless fingers, bouncing off my bare toes and skidding across the carpet. I froze where I was, my heart thumping in my chest so hard I heard the whoosh of blood in my ears.

Panic shot ice down my spine.

My nerves screamed: DANGER! DANGER!

Head spinning with fear, I tried to think. The long, hard

body pressed to my back made that impossible. Eyes squeezed tightly shut, memories flashed against my closed lids in a staccato beat of everything I wanted to forget.

Hard hands grabbing me in the dark. The weight of a body, so much bigger than mine. Pain.

It isn't Anthony, I told myself. *Anthony is dead.*

Summoning every ounce of courage I had, I said, "Let me go."

A low, husky voice rumbled in my ear. "Not until you tell me what the hell you're doing in here in the middle of the night."

A hitch in my voice, I said, "Amelia. Amelia sent me."

The words tangled in my throat. I couldn't say more. The heat of a male body so close to mine, the strength of his arms closing me in, his warm breath against my cheek - it was too much.

I hadn't been this close to a man, any man, since my husband had died.

After Anthony, I'd never wanted to be this close to a man again.

In a rush of awareness, I knew this wasn't Aiden. Aiden had always been careful to preserve a polite, formal distance between us. If he caught me skulking around the house in the middle of the night, he'd never grab me from behind. Heck, with the way Aiden adored Amelia he'd probably volunteer to finish the prank himself.

If it wasn't Aiden. It had to be Gage. Aiden's cousin had arrived the day before, when Amelia and I had been out on a shopping trip, picking up construction paper and tape. Gage hadn't joined the family for dinner.

Hoping my guess was right, I said, "I'm Sophie. Amelia's nurse."

A grunt in my ear, but the arms around me didn't

loosen. Shoot. I knew better than to struggle. Fighting back only made them hurt you more. My breath shallow, body still, I tried again.

"I'm allowed to be here. I'm not doing anything wrong. Please let me go."

I felt his head drop to my shoulder, the heat of his forehead pressing into my bare neck. He drew in a deep breath.

Was he smelling me?

Panic sliced through me again.

No. Please, no. Please don't make me have to leave this place. I'd thought I was safe here. For the first time in years, I was safe. I didn't want to have to leave.

His heart jackhammered, the echo of its frantic beats fluttering against my back where his chest pressed tightly to me.

"Please," I whispered. The arms around me loosened. I stayed frozen. I was too cautious to move until I'd truly been set free. This could be a trap and I was too smart to fall for it. Anthony had trained me well.

Warm lips brushed the side of my neck. Another deep inhale. He *was* smelling me. The urge to flee was almost impossible to resist, but I knew in my gut that running was the worst mistake I could make.

I wracked my brain for everything I knew of Gage. He was the oldest son of James and Anna Winters, Aiden's aunt and uncle. James and Anna had been brutally murdered when Gage was a child. When Aiden's parents had been killed in an identical crime eight years later, Gage had been eighteen. The day after their funeral he'd joined the army. Until today, he'd never really come home.

Details of his military service were scarce, but Amelia had told me everything she knew. He'd enlisted, gone to college, then through officer training school, before he'd joined the Rangers. After that he'd moved into special forces, his missions and teams so top secret his family hadn't been sure he was still with the army until they'd called to tell Aiden that Gage was missing.

For months the family had been stuck in limbo, swinging between grief and hope, right up until a second call had informed Aiden that Gage had escaped captivity. He was coming home as soon as the military hospital released him, but they'd warned Aiden that the months of imprisonment had taken a toll.

Gage was no longer the man his family remembered.

Aiden had commented dryly that Gage had been gone so long, they barely knew him at all. No matter what the circumstances of his homecoming, to his family, Gage was a stranger. As my panic ebbed, I realized the man holding me captive might possibly be more freaked out than I was.

He probably had some form of post traumatic stress if he'd really been held captive for months. Finding an intruder in his home was just the kind of thing that would set him off, especially when his home must seem like a foreign place after so many years away.

Logic told me that a former special forces soldier suffering from PTSD was *more* dangerous, not less, but my guess at what might be going through his head put me back in control. As a woman alone in the dark, I was terrified. As a nurse, and a woman used to dealing with volatile men, I knew what I needed to do.

"Gage?" I asked, careful to keep my voice low and soothing. "Gage, it's okay. You can let go. I'm Amelia's nurse. I'm allowed to be here. It's okay."

I kept talking in the same soothing voice, feeling the tension slip from his body. Eventually, he lifted his head and stepped back, setting me free. With an odd sense of triumph, I crossed the room before I turned around. I thought he was steady, but I wanted some space between us, just in case.

"I'm going to turn on the lamp," I warned just before I reached beneath the shade and turned the knob. Light flared, blinding me for a moment. A deep chuckle rumbled from across the room.

"Whose idea was it?" he asked.

His voice distracted me for a second, so deep and calm, at odds with the tension that had seized his muscles only a few minutes before. I glanced at the light and saw the shadow of an enormous spider lurking on the inside of the shade. I stepped away with a shiver before I realized what I was doing. Silly, since I was the one who had taped the bugs in place, but I hadn't expected them to look so real. Amelia was good.

Clearing my throat, I said, "Amelia's. It's always Amelia's idea." I wanted to ask if he was okay, but I held my tongue.

"Clever," he said.

"That's Amelia," I agreed.

"Is this the only room you did?"

"It is." Judging it safe to move, I began to gather up my materials, tucking my phone back in the pocket of my robe and making sure I had all the extra bugs and the tape. A prank was no good if I left the evidence sitting around.

"Mrs. W won't be happy."

I smiled. It was sweet the way the family doted on Mrs. W. I'd always imagined a family as wealthy and powerful as the Winters would be stuffy, far above those they'd consider the help. Instead they treated Mrs. W like family and had welcomed me as an equal, insisting I join them for meals and giving me a room in the main house that was bigger than my apartment when I'd been in nursing school.

"I already texted her," I reassured Gage. "She'll make a big fuss tomorrow when she turns on the lights. Unless Aiden does it first."

"Aiden doesn't know?"

I shook my head, picking up the last scrap of construction paper. Suddenly without anything to do, I crossed my arms over my chest. Gage stood in shadow, his features hard to make out, but I was uncomfortably aware I was standing there in my robe, my hair down, looking like an unprofessional mess.

In the six months I'd been living in Winters House I'd never encountered another soul awake in the middle of the night.

Clearing my throat, I said, "No, Aiden likes to be surprised."

Gage let out a grunt I couldn't decipher. He took a step forward, leaving the shadows of the corner. Light bathed his features and I lost my breath. I'd heard Gage and Aiden were like twins. Everyone else must be blind. To my eyes, they looked nothing alike.

Sure, they both had the same build - tall, broad shoulders, lean hips. The same dark hair. Even their features were superficially similar, with sharp cheekbones, aristocratic noses and full lower lips. Where Aiden's hair had the same auburn tones as his little sister, Charlie, Gage's was a true brown, not a hint of red to be seen.

I'd always thought soldiers wore their hair short, but Gage's was a little long. Shaggy. As if he hadn't had it cut in months. Which of course, he hadn't. I imagined his hairstyle hadn't been a priority when he'd been trying to escape his captors.

He'd probably cut it now that he was home. Maybe with shorter hair he'd look more like Aiden. I took in the tension in his shoulders, his hands curled into fists.

No. The obvious aside, Aiden looked nothing like Gage. His haircut had nothing to do with it.

Aiden was cool. Refined. Controlled.

Standing in the pool of light, his faded grey t-shirt stretched around his biceps, hugging his well defined chest, Gage was raw, his power barely leashed. Despite his stillness, he vibrated with energy. I sensed it was taking everything he had to remain where he was. His vivid blue eyes were the least of the differences between Gage and his cousin.

Those eyes were leveled on me, pinning me in place as effectively as his arms had a few minutes before.

Clearing my throat, I said, "Are you going to spoil it for her?"

"The prank?" Gage asked. At my nod, he said, "No."

"Thank you." I started for the door to the library, careful to give Gage a wide berth. I didn't think he was going to grab me again, but it seemed smarter to stay out of arm's reach.

"Tell me next time," he said.

"What?" I stopped at the door, confused.

He was silent for a long moment before answering in a halting voice. "I don't do well with surprises these days. The next time Amelia decides to mess with us, fill me in."

Instantly, I understood. Amelia's plan to duct tape an airhorn to Aiden's desk chair would be a nightmare to a man newly home from a combat zone, even if he *didn't* have post-traumatic stress and I was betting Gage did.

"Do you have a cell?" I asked.

Gage raised his eyebrows in question. I explained, "I

text Mrs. W to warn her. I'll try to talk Amelia out of a few of her plans that might be a problem, but I can text you, too. That way you know what's coming."

"So, Amelia hasn't slowed down. Good to know some things don't change," he said, his voice heavy with something I couldn't quite identify. Regret? Whatever it was, Gage Winters sounded sad.

I had the absurd urge to comfort him.

Absurd because not only did I not know what was wrong, he was a Winters. Yes, he'd been through a terrible experience. But he was alive. He was home with his family, living in this enormous mansion, with a job waiting for him at Winters Incorporated, and more money than he could count stashed away in the bank.

Gage Winters didn't need my comfort. He didn't need anything from me.

He might remind me of a wounded animal, but wounded animals were dangerous. And I'd been bitten enough.

The only person in this house who needs you is Amelia, I reminded myself. *Stay away from Gage Winters.*

"Are you in Vance's old room?" Gage asked.

"I am. Across from Amelia. I guess her room used to be Holden and Tate's?"

Gage nodded. "If you're done with your bugs, I'll walk you back."

"It's just down the hall," I protested.

"All the same. I'll walk you back."

I didn't bother to argue. Gage followed me out the door, turning off the lamp before we left the room. The short stretch of hall outside the library was dark, the doors to the wine room and Aiden's office lost in the shadows.

We turned the corner to the main hall where silvery

moonlight streamed through the tall, arched windows, casting the walls in dreamlike shades. Outside the arched windows, in the center courtyard of Winters House, a fountain burbled, the water flashing black and silver.

I loved this house. It belonged in a fairy tale. I completely understood why Mrs. W was so devoted to it. How could Gage have left this place and not come back for so many years? In the six months I'd been with Amelia, Winters House had become a haven.

Why had Gage left it just when he'd needed it most?

I couldn't imagine the losses this family had suffered. Not really. I'd lost my mother to cancer when I was a teenager, but Gage had not only lost both his parents as a child, he'd lost the aunt and uncle who had raised him when he'd barely been a man.

More than once since he'd gone missing I'd wondered what had happened to make the eighteen year old Gage flee his family home.

Now that he was back, was he going to stay? None of it was my business, but I couldn't help my curiosity.

Gage kept his distance as we walked down the hall, following just slightly behind me. Our feet shuffled along the polished hardwood floors, almost silent in the sleeping house. This wasn't the first time I'd wandered Winters House in the middle of the night, but it was the first time I'd done so with company.

We reached the door to my bedroom, opposite the hall from Amelia's. I reached for the handle, and Gage's fingers closed over mine. I started in surprise, letting out a little squeak. I was grateful for the dark as I felt my cheeks turn red.

"I'm sorry about earlier," Gage said in his low rumble. "I

wasn't expecting to see anyone in the library and I reacted on instinct. I didn't mean to scare you."

"You didn't," I lied. "It's okay."

Gage dropped his hand and stared at me, his blue eyes gleaming in the moonlight, seeing everything. He knew I was lying, knew I'd been scared. Lips pressed together and eyes wide, I silently begged him to let it go.

Gage took a step back and dropped his hand.

"Sleep well, Sophie," he said, his low voice sending shivers down my spine.

"You, too," I whispered, and escaped into my room.

Click Here to read The Billionaire's Angel

Also by Ivy L~~

**Don't Miss Out on New Relea~~
Giveaways, and More!!**

Join Ivy's Readers Group @ ivylayne.com/readers

THE HEARTS OF SAWYERS BEND

Stolen Heart

Sweet Heart

Scheming Heart

Rebel Heart

Wicked Heart

THE UNTANGLED SERIES

Unraveled

Undone

Uncovered

THE WINTERS SAGA

The Billionaire's Secret Heart (Novella)

The Billionaire's Secret Love (Novella)

The Billionaire's Pet

The Billionaire's Promise

ABOUT IVY LAYNE

Ivy Layne has had her nose stuck in a book since she first learned to decipher the English language. Sometime in her early teens, she stumbled across her first Romance, and the die was cast. Though she pretended to pay attention to her creative writing professors, she dreamed of writing steamy romance instead of literary fiction. These days, she's neck deep in alpha heroes and the smart, sexy women who love them.

Married to her very own alpha hero (who rubs her back after a long day of typing, but also leaves his socks on the floor). Ivy lives in the mountains of North Carolina where she and her other half are having a blast raising two energetic little boys. Aside from her family, Ivy's greatest loves are coffee and chocolate, preferably together.

VISIT IVY
Facebook.com/AuthorIvyLayne
Instagram.com/authorivylayne/
www.ivylayne.com
books@ivylayne.com

Made in the USA
Middletown, DE
13 January 2024

47794303R00097